THE BRITTLER SISTERS
BOOK FOUR

USA *TODAY* BESTSELLING AUTHOR

JOSEPHINE BLAKE

Chapter One

Long Island, New York
Summer, 1885

Sarah

The structure sat tucked away and forgotten on a lonely ridge overlooking the Atlantic. Its crumbling walls looked as though they might be blown away by a strong breeze. Sarah had never learned the real history of the place. Some days, she thought the remains must have been a monastery from the early 16th century, left by monks who'd abandoned it in favor of a more sheltered climate. On other days she knew it to be the magnificent home of an ancient warlord and his beautiful wife, guarding over the territory that they had conquered together.

Today, it was a home. Each stone had been carefully stacked upon the other to provide the sturdiest of shelters.

The windows were chosen to offer the spectacular views of the ocean beyond.

Every bit of this was pure fantasy, however. Whatever the building had once been, nature had reduced it to nothing more than a precarious pile of stones and rubble. While most of the walls still stood, supports lay slanted sideways, and the ceiling had long since caved in.

Sarah ran her fingertips over the dust-smeared walls as she carefully negotiated a path up the deteriorated stairs. On the landing ahead, her window beckoned. Her most cherished place in all the world. On her right hand, a gaping hole in the floor displayed a startling glimpse of the lower level. Fragments of rock and fallen stone decorated the ground here, putting Sarah-Jane in mind of a cemetery. But it was in a peaceful sort of way. They rested like fallen soldiers, watching her with a detached sort of curiosity, their duties done.

Glaring, opaline skies spread out over Sarah's head. Seagulls danced and screamed, twirling in the wind.

At last, she mounted the final stair and stood still for a moment, looking around with a contented smile on her face. She'd stumbled across this place quite by accident a few months previously, and had been returning to the ruins on a regular basis ever since. It was a blessed reprieve from the hustle and bustle of Manhattan, where you were lucky not to be cast into the street and trodden underfoot by the various passers-by. The people of Manhattan were often so determined to get where they were headed, they would not even pause to apologize if they knocked you sideways into a fruit stand.

Kicking aside pebbles, Sarah approached the large hole in the wall across the landing. She supposed it had once been a window, but now the frame had crumbled away, leaving nothing but a semi-rectangular shape in the decaying rampart.

The ocean stretched out before her, lapping at the rocky cliffs below. It was a particularly fine day. The sun was shining on the back of her neck and a light breeze tickled the light hairs there.

Sarah leaned against the stone wall for a moment, her blue eyes scanning the horizon. Occasionally during these little forays, she'd seen a sailboat pass by, but otherwise, her little patch of heaven was quite undisturbed. She liked it that way.

It wasn't exactly what you would call normal. Well-to-do members of New York society didn't often scale dilapidated buildings on the outer coast. In fact, Sarah smiled at the thought of the look that would come over her mother's face if she ever found out what Sarah was really doing when she was supposed to be on an afternoon ride through the nearby park.

She glanced over the edge of the landing at her steed, a pretty, chocolate colored mare by the name of Averleigh.

Averleigh was munching happily on a patch of grass, her long, black tail swooshing behind her. Sarah shook her head. Her horse was energetic and explorative, and she never passed up an opportunity to eat. Sarah never bothered to tie her up. She merely led Averleigh to the nearest patch of grass and let her graze.

The sun had crawled lower in the sky now, drifting closer to the place where the waves met the clouds. Sarah sighed. She'd been here nearly a half an hour already, and this spot wasn't exactly just a jaunt outside the front door of the Brittler's summer cottage. She had to ride an hour along the coastline to get here. But as the sun began to sink into the ocean, crimson streaks slid across the sky as though an invisible hand was stroking over the remaining clouds with a paintbrush. She couldn't justify leaving now. Not with the magnificent display that was unfolding before her.

Knowing perfectly well that she would regret choosing to stay as she endured her mother's remonstrations that night, Sarah lifted her skirts and clambered onto the window ledge. She felt joyously free here. Free from the routine, and from the constraints of her daily life.

Her mind wandered ceaselessly as her ankles dangled in the open air. A few hundred feet below her, the waves of the Atlantic carved a path into the high cliffs. Sarah had seen the sunset here before, twice in past years, but it never failed to amaze her. It looked as though the sun was a portal, sucking all light from the sky. Above her head, deep navies were fading into purples, the purples fading into blacks. Sarah tilted her head back to see if she could make out any stars hovering over her head. It was then, as her neck stretched and her shoulders tautened, that she heard a small cough.

Sarah whipped her head around. The shadowy crevices of the ruins suddenly looked forbidding. She peered into them, trying to decide if the noise she had heard was just Averleigh, snuffling in the long grass. Her body had stilled, like a rabbit scenting a predator. She was listening hard, but whether because the crashing waves were drowning out the noise, or because there had never been any at all, it did not come again. Deciding that what she had heard had indeed been her horse, she shifted around to catch sight of the last vestiges of light sinking beneath the waves. There was a final gleam and a flash of orange, then darkness began sliding onto the sun's vacant throne.

Sarah sighed again. Twisting around in her seat, already dreading the telling off she was bound to receive when she arrived home, she made to climb off her perch.

"What are you doing?"

Sarah gasped. Her grip slipped on the rough stone. Then she was tilting backward. Her heavy skirts tumbled over the stone ledge. She was falling.

Sarah let out a cry as she was pitched sideways, her fingers grappling at the crumbling stone around her. All she could hear was the sound of the swelling waves. They would be the last thing she ever heard.

A hand, warm, dry and masculine, shot out of the window and took hold of her dress. There was a grunt, a sputter, and a soft curse. Then Sarah felt herself yanked forward. She cried out, and then she landed painfully on the stone ledge. The man holding her gave another heave, and her legs slid onto the landing.

"What in the blazes?!" her rescuer was shouting, his voice seemed rather hoarse, and she thought she detected a British accent. Sarah straightened up, coughing. She'd landed hard on the stone, and a rough boulder had caught her in the midriff.

"I might ask you the same question!" she gasped through a moan as she pressed a hand to her stomach.

"No, you bloody well will not!" The man was climbing to his feet now, and even in the pressing darkness, Sarah could tell how very tall he was. "What are you doing here? Who are you?"

"Who are you?!" demanded Sarah, offended. She sat on the ground a moment longer, still trying to catch her breath.

"Williamson," he growled. "Carson Williamson. What are you doing on my land?"

"Your land?" Sarah sniffed. "Nobody lives here." She ignored the hand Carson Williamson was offering to her and used the nearby wall for support as she stood.

"Not for some time, no," said Carson. "And certainly not, here." He looked around the crumbling structure with a look of utmost disgust on his face. "But I've just purchased this property from the city."

"Is that so?"

"Yes, it is," said Carson, looking nettled.

Now that she was facing him, Sarah couldn't help but notice that Carson Williamson was quite good looking. He had the square jaw and high brow that was so often admired by the other girls her age. With his wind-swept hair and his tall collar, he looked very much like the captain of the Queen's fleet. His hair was dark, and he wore it trimmed short, as though he had no time for such frivolous things as hair combing.

Sarah closed her eyes and shook her head. Partially to rid herself of his startling image, but mostly to convey amused skepticism.

"Well, I thank you for saving me. Although, I might point out that I may not have required saving had you not crept up behind me like a common sneak thief." Sarah dusted a hand over her skirts irritably. The night was truly upon them now. The skies had gone black, tinged with purple on the distant horizon, and stars were beginning to peer out at them from their soft blanket of darkness. If she delayed setting out any longer, her father would send out a search party before she could return home.

Carson looked furious. "You may not have needed saving?" he growled, taking a menacing step nearer to her. "You looked as though you were readying to toss yourself to the waves!"

"What?!" cried Sarah, exasperated now. "I was watching the sunset." She gestured vaguely out of her window.

"You were going to do it, weren't you?!" Carson accused, waving his hands. "You were going to jump."

"Preposterous!" shouted Sarah. "I've no desire to end my life, and your insinuation proves that you are someone with whom I would rather not spend another moment of it." Furious, Sarah stalked around the man, heading for the stairs that led down to the lower level. But to her chagrin, Carson seized hold of her wrist as she passed. "Unhand me, you heathen!" she squawked, struggling, but his grip was like iron.

"I can't let you go." He said, a look of utter determination sliding across his shadowed face. "What's to stop you from trying again the moment you are out of my sight? I'm taking you to the police station."

"You'll do nothing of the sort!"

"I can and I will. You're trespassing!"

Sarah froze, her mind whirring frantically. She took a deep breath. "I wasn't trying to kill myself," she insisted. "The thought never crossed my mind. I'm quite happy, actually," she said.

"You're lying," barked Carson. "That is precisely the sort of thing a woman of ill mental constitution would say."

Sarah rolled her eyes. "It is also the sort of thing a woman would say if she were telling the truth."

"Rubbish." Carson Williamson took a firmer grip on her wrist and began shunting her toward the stairs.

"This is ridiculous," Sarah cried desperately. "I only came here to—" she broke off. She had the distinct feeling that nothing she could say would make the slightest bit of difference. She let the tension leave her arms. "Fine," she said at last. "Fine. I'll go with you. But only so that I can explain exactly what did happen to the constable. You'll see. In a few hours' time, you'll be offering me an apology." It was a trick. She had absolutely no intention of being taken to the authorities. The resulting scandal would give her mother heart failure.

Carson Williamson snorted. What little light that was left was disappearing fast. Sarah clicked her tongue for Averleigh, and her horse came trotting up to meet her, shaking her magnificent mane.

Carson halted, deliberating. Against the far wall, Sarah could make out a second horse, but only because its pelt was white as snow against the backdrop of shadow. Fabulous, she thought. Here comes my hero, riding in on a white horse. She shook her head again.

Her captor seemed to have reached a decision. "You'll ride with me on my horse. That way you can't escape."

"Escape?" laughed Sarah, as though the idea was far from her mind, although she was even now testing the pressure of his grip. Perhaps if she took him off guard? "Why on Earth would I want to escape from a strapping young man such as yourself?" she purred suddenly.

Carson looked down at her, apparently taken aback. Sarah certainly hoped so. It was getting harder and harder to make out his fine features in the dark. She pressed her advantage. "I mean," she said softly, coming a bit closer to him so that she could smell the faint scent of warm leather and whiskey that seemed to emanate from his skin. "I'm sure there's not a woman alive who would mind being imprisoned by the likes of you."

He must have a fantastic ego if this is having any effect on him at all, thought Sarah. She pursed her lips and pressed closer to him still, coming right up to his chest and smiling coyly up at him.

"Err..." Carson seemed a little lost for words. He was staring down at her in confusion, and Sarah felt his grip on her slacken. In one swift movement, she raised her foot and kicked him hard in the shins. Carson dropped like a stone and Sarah broke free of his grasp. In a whirl of satin skirts, she leaped onto her horse's back and kicked Averleigh forward. Only remembering to duck in the very last second, so that she felt the top of her head brush the open stone archway as her horse bolted out of the ruins and flew into the night.

She arrived at the summer estate an hour later, her heartbeat having just returned to a semi-normal pace. "There you are, Miss Sarah!" cried the groom, his expression looking a bit wild. "Your father only just headed out looking for you. I'll ride into town and bring him back straight away."

Sarah groaned. "Thank you, Kincaid," she muttered, swiping her hair out of her face as she dismounted. She gave her horse a grateful pat. "Well done, Averleigh. Well done, girl." Her horse's flanks heaved in a disgruntled sigh, and Sarah kissed her velvety nose before turning to head into the house.

She set her shoulders as she entered through a side door, kicking off her riding boots. Predictably, her mother was on her before she'd even had a chance to catch her breath. Samantha Brittler was a thin woman, with her hair in a tight bun at the base of her neck. She looked something like a well-dressed, well-versed Sunday school teacher. One who might wrap your knuckles with a ruler if you scrolled your *S* backward on accident.

"Where have you been? Do you have any idea how worried we all were?"

"Mother," sighed Sarah. "I'm quite alright." She shrugged out of her coat and hung it on an iron peg in the hall.

"What happened?"

"Averleigh threw a shoe," said Sarah dismissively as she slid around her mother and through the tiny gap she had left in the doorway behind her.

"Don't give me that tosh," snapped Samantha. She stalked after her daughter, her skirts swishing around her ankles. "You've been gone at least half the day."

Sarah shrugged, still moving toward the kitchen. "It was a pleasant day."

"There's a difference in spending the day riding and returning well before sunset, and staying out until all hours of the night!"

"Really, Mother. It's hardly eight."

"We thought you'd been kidnapped."

"You mean that you thought I'd been kidnapped. I don't see any other members of our family making such a fuss."

"Your father's gone out to look for you."

"Well," said Sarah, bumping open the kitchen door with her hip. "He won't be able to find me."

Samantha sniffed. "Obviously," she said with distaste.

Sarah turned away from her mother as she entered the kitchen. Unsurprisingly, she found Noelle there, bent over a cookbook, with the cook, Marcia, hovering over her like an anxious goose.

"Oh, there you are, are you?" said Marcia, glancing up to see who would dare to enter her domain. "You've had us all in a right flap, Miss Sarah," she said disapprovingly.

"Honestly," muttered Sarah, sinking down across from her sister at the tiny kitchen table. Noelle peered up at her through a pair of round spectacles perched on the end of her nose.

"So," she said, her eyes shifting between her mother and her sister. "Where was she?"

"She says her horse threw a shoe," muttered Samantha, still glaring down at the top of Sarah's head. They spoke as if she wasn't in the room at all.

Noelle turned back to her recipes. "Hmmm," was all she said.

Marcia had been puttering around on the other side of the room. A moment later, she plunked a steaming bowl of soup and a fresh slice of bread down in front of Sarah.

"You missed dinner," she said saucily, as though Sarah had disturbed her on some moral level for daring to miss one of her meals.

"Did I?" asked Sarah sarcastically. Choosing to ignore the reproving glares of every woman in the room, she thanked Marcia grudgingly and tucked into her soup.

Her mother and Marcia watched her, both with identical looks of annoyance creasing their brows.

"This puff pastry, Marcia," said Noelle, who was clearly more interested in her cookbook than making Sarah feel bad for being a few hours late getting home. "Is it something you knead well, or do you let the bits of shortening be if they wish."

"You must knead them out, dear," said Marcia fondly, turning dewy eyes on her young protégé.

Noelle nodded absently. The silence that followed was stony. Their mother had taken up an elegant perch on a barstool and was now looking out the kitchen window into the dark garden. She looked rather different than she usually did, surrounded by the clutter of the beach front kitchen. Used to organizing one of the largest and grandest houses in Manhattan, Sarah supposed her mother might not have been quite as angry with her if she wasn't so frustrated with her lack of responsibilities.

Her father had purchased the summer cottage a few years previously, and maintained that the entire family should join him there for the races each year since. Sarah loved it. It was quieter here, away from the hustle and bustle of Manhattan. There was room to stretch, room to breathe, and her normal restrictions in the city were lessened here, away from the prying eyes of the neighbors.

The firelight from the wood stove flickered, and the quiet was broken by the echoing bang of the front door flying open. "Oh good," said Samantha vindictively. "Your father's home." She cast a furious glance at Sarah and, sure enough, a moment later, Sarah winced as her father's voice echoed off the walls in the foyer.

"Sarah-Jane!"

Sarah patted her lips with her napkin and stood. "Thank you, again, for saving me something, Marcia."

Marcia humphed and whisked away her bowl, but the look in her eyes was rather pitying as Thomas Brittler's voice rang through the house again.

"Sarah! Get in here!"

Sarah sighed and left the room in search of her father, and the firm reprimand she knew was in store for her.

"Nothing," Thomas Brittler said as Sarah entered the downstairs parlor, "gives you the right to be out without an escort, especially not after dark."

"But I—"

Thomas held up a hand, and Sarah fell into a respectful—slightly disgruntled—silence.

Her father was a thin man, with a long, clever face and a spectacular mustache. He appeared younger than his fifty-two years and exhibited a great vitality that was difficult to match, even for his children. Although he was well-built, giving him the sturdy appearance of a race horse, his waistcoat was looking a little snug across his stomach these days.

"Don't you realize how irresponsible this was?" he asked, looking her directly in the eye. "Quite apart from the appearance of the thing, it's very dangerous. What were you thinking?"

Lying to her father wasn't quite like lying to anyone else. He looked so very disappointed in her that Sarah felt the guilt of what she had done settle down on her shoulders like a shroud.

"I'm sorry," she whispered quietly with a small shrug. "I wasn't thinking."

"Apparently not," growled her father, looking highly frustrated. He frowned as he stomped across the room in search of his cigar case.

"You're not to be riding for a few weeks," he said. He retrieved his cigars and spun to face her.

"Oh, but what about—"

"The race?" finished Thomas, clipping the end of his cigar. He eyed Sarah as he struck a match and held it to the end. "Perhaps staying behind with your sisters will give you some time to think. You've had quite enough freedoms over the last few days."

"But, Father..." whined Sarah. She'd been looking forward to escorting Averleigh to the racetrack at Brighton Beach, where she was known for her speed and agility. Her horse was a gorgeous thoroughbred, with a talent for racing that was often remarked upon, and even more often, bet upon by New York's high society.

Thomas Brittler held up his hand again. Sarah fell into a bristling silence, not daring to contradict him.

"Perhaps sitting out this event will enable you to see my point. In the very least, it should make you think twice before you decide to neglect your good sense." He nodded sharply, evidently pleased with his decision, and then sat down in his armchair, facing the fire, his cigar clamped between his teeth.

Sarah opened her mouth to plead her case once more, but at a swift glare from her father, she closed it again.

"Be a help to your mother over these next couple weeks," he said in an unmistakable tone of finality. Sarah nodded, trying not to cry, and knew herself to be dismissed.

Chapter Two

"WELL, YOU WERE QUITE late," said Dianna, looking up from her writing desk as Sarah-Jane collapsed on her bed. "And you didn't bother to take an escort."

"It wasn't my fault!" Sarah exclaimed, tossing her arms and legs into the air.

"Really?" chuckled Dianna, amused. "Whose fault was it then?"

"It was that wretched man!"

Sarah heard her sister's hand still on the parchment. Still holding her fountain pen aloft, Dianna looked around suspiciously. "What man?"

Sarah sighed, already regretting the slip of her tongue, and turned her head sideways on her sister's bed to look at her.

Dianna eyed her for a moment, waiting for her to speak, and when Sarah didn't move, she screwed the cap back onto her pen. With the ink still shining on her paper, she picked it up, blew on it softly and then tucked it into her nightstand, locking the drawer with a small key around her neck.

"What was that?" asked Sarah curiously.

"Just a letter to a friend," said Dianna dismissively. Sarah got the distinct impression that she wasn't alone in concealing things at the moment, and was about to prod Dianna further when her sister turned and plopped herself down on the bed next to her.

"What man?" she asked again, this time firmly, and Sarah knew that there would be no distracting her. Dianna was like a hound. When she caught a scent, she wasn't going to give up until she found its source.

Sarah sat up and avoided her sister's eyes. "He's no one. He's... he shouldn't have been there at all."

Dianna promptly moved around to the other side of the bed, trying to get a good look at Sarah's face. When Sarah still wouldn't meet her eyes, she took hold of her chin between her thumb and forefinger and forced Sarah's gaze into her own. "Tell me what happened," she said sourly.

Sarah jerked her face away from Dianna's fingers. "Don't treat me like a child, Di."

"Don't act like one."

The sisters glared at one another, and as usual, Sarah caved first.

"I didn't go to Helmsley Park," she said in defeat, her body going limp. Dianna raised her eyebrows but didn't say anything. "I've only ever gone for a ride in the park once," she admitted.

"Oh really," said Dianna, and her tone made it evident that this was not a revelation to her. She sat herself down on the bed, displacing the many pillows at the head, and pulling one of the largest into her lap. The posture was very familiar to Sarah. Dianna was readying herself to listen to her story, as was their custom.

"I've been riding the coastline," Sarah started. She was playing with a loose string on Dianna's coverlet. After a moment, she chanced a peek at Dianna through her eyelashes.

"Alone, I take it?" asked Dianna. She didn't sound disgruntled, merely resigned. "Why?"

"I was at the Devons' for lunch a few weeks ago... and afterward, we went out riding."

"Okay...?"

"There was a moment where Tabitha and I were separated, and Averleigh and I had to follow the coastline to return to their house."

"That doesn't really explain why you've insisted on doing so every week since," grumbled Dianna. She crossed her arms over her pillow, still watching Sarah expectantly.

Sarah smiled as she recalled the first moment she had set eyes on the ruins, towering above the ocean like a magnificent palace in the clouds.

"I found this place, Di. This amazing place."

"What is it? A gambling hall?"

Sarah laughed out loud at this.

"Well, that's the only reason I could think of that you might need to return to the same place over and over again. Have you paid off your debts? Is there more to come?" Dianna was chuckling now. She gave Sarah a playful dig in the ribs. "So, what is it then?"

Sarah paused to think for a moment. "I don't really know what it is. That is," she continued hurriedly as Dianna's face darkened. "I don't know what it used to be. It's... a ruin, of sorts..." she drifted off, shrugging her slender shoulders.

"You've been riding along the New York coastline for hours, once a week, to visit a ruin?" said Dianna incredulously.

"It's not just that," Sarah hedged. She climbed to her feet and strode over to Dianna's bedroom window. The sky beyond it was now an inky black. "It's just a bit... just a bit calmer there, you know?"

Dianna paused. "You sound like me," she said at last.

"Everything is just so...crowded. So structured. It feels good to sneak away for a while."

Dianna's eyes had clouded over. Sarah got the impression that she had lost her sister to some far off land. "Yes, I know what you mean," she said, quietly. "It would be nice to get away from it all, wouldn't it?"

"It is," whispered Sarah. "It's wonderful." She sighed. "It's not just the ruin though, it's the ride getting there. Averleigh can move in the open, I feel like she looks forward to it as much as I do."

Dianna smiled. "I suppose she enjoys getting off the track once in a while."

Sarah nodded sadly, and then she sank dejectedly onto the rocking chair beside the window. "Father says I'm not allowed to go to the race on Saturday," she whispered.

Dianna looked at her, long and hard, as though she was trying to decide if she approved of this or not. Apparently, she decided she did not. "I'll try to talk to him."

Sarah felt a hopeful bubble inflate itself from within the pit of her misery. "Oh, would you?" If anyone could bring her father around, it was Di.

Dianna smiled again. "Of course," she said, and then her brow furrowed. "If you agree never to stay out this late again. You know how Mother gets. She was ready to send Father for the constable."

Sarah nodded rapidly. "I'll be more careful," she said.

"Besides," Dianna's lips quirked up in the corner. "You really shouldn't miss Averleigh's first race of the season."

It wasn't until she was lying in bed, several hours later, that Sarah realized she had managed to distract Dianna after all. They had both forgotten all about Carson Williamson.

The next day dawned, foggy and bright, so when Sarah looked out of her ground floor window, all she could make out was a pale, incandescent gleam. By mid-morning, however, the fog had burnt away to be replaced by a truly glorious burst of sunshine. In the air, there was the whisper of salt and sea.

Sarah made her way down the hall and slid into a seat at the dining room table for breakfast alongside her sisters.

"M-morning, Sarah," said Dianna through a wide yawn.

Sarah smiled at her, taking notice of the dark circles beneath her sister's eyes. "You look like you've been through the mill," she said, matter-of-factly. "Did you sleep alright?"

"What? Oh, yes, I slept fine." For some strange reason, Dianna's cheeks had colored. Sarah eyed her curiously.

"What are you all up to today?" asked their father from the head of the table. His voice was slightly muffled by the large newspaper he held in front of his face.

Sarah wondered if he was still furious with her.

"I was thinking I'd take 'Elle down to the beach," said Charlotte, tapping her spoon on a hard boiled egg.

"What?" cried Noelle in dismay. "I hate the sand."

"You need some sunshine," said Charlotte, glaring at their youngest sister. All you do is skulk down in the kitchen and pour over those old cookbooks."

"I think your sister's right, Noelle," said Thomas Brittler. Why don't you spend some time by the waves? In fact," he added, turning a stony gaze onto Sarah, "why don't you all go?"

Sarah frowned. She'd intended to visit the stables to check on Averleigh and then head to the shops with Dianna. She had the impression that her father was trying to keep her as far from her horse as possible at the moment, and the thought irked her to no end. She said nothing though, and breakfast finished on a rather quiet note.

The beach was thronging with the wealthy members of New York society. The sky above them was a clear, pale blue, and the waves shone pearl bright in the sunlight. Each of the Brittler girls wore a wide bonnet and shielded their pale skin from the sun with a light parasol.

Sarah bobbed along a little behind her sisters, eyeing the beach populace with a practiced eye. A few steps ahead of her, the back of Charlotte's neck was growing steadily pinker as they walked.

"Keep up, you," she said cheerfully, slowing her pace to link her arm with Sarah's.

Sarah scowled at her sister as two men cantered by on horseback, doffing their hats to the sisters as they passed.

"I don't understand why so many people insist on flocking to the shores. It's not as though many actually get into the water."

"Maybe they just enjoy the view," said Charlotte, failing to be deflected by Sarah's foul mood.

"I could do without the sight of Miss Carlisle's tasteless displays, although I daresay many of the gentlemen would be disappointed if she were not present."

Charlotte turned to look in the direction Sarah had indicated. Miss Eliza Carlisle, the daughter of a well-respected and profitable department store owner, was flouncing across the sand in a low-cut, off the shoulder bathing costume that would surely not manage to cling to her sumptuous form if she were to submerge herself in the ocean. The thing appeared ready to give way, a fact that most of the gentlemen on the beach seemed to have noticed.

Charlotte rolled her eyes and growled deep in her throat. "That woman is a menace," she said quietly. "No one wants their child to think that sort of behavior is acceptable, and the men... well, just look at them. They're half-tripping over themselves just to have a look at her. It's as though the beach has suddenly become a bawdy show at Miss Divencio's."

Sarah laughed. It really wasn't quite as bad as all that. But... she had to agree with her sister. Most of the men were sneaking glances out of the corners of their eyes, and a few had even come to a halt, watching Miss Carlisle with undisguised interest.

There was one man, however, standing a little ways off, that did not seem at all pleased with the exhibition. His lip was curled in distaste, and he had turned resolutely away from the rest, his frown evident.

Before Sarah knew what she was doing, she had taken hold of Charlotte's arm and shoved her sister in front of herself, pulling her bonnet low over her face, and twirling her parasol down to shield her from Carson Williamson's line of sight.

"Sarah, what are you...?"

"Shh," Sarah hissed. "Walk. Just walk. Don't let him see me."

"Don't let who—?"

"Charlotte Elaine Brittler, I beg of you, do not draw any attention to me."

Her sister could not mistake the urgency in her voice. "Very well," she said, "but you will explain, won't you?"

Sarah didn't answer, she was too fixated on peering through the lace of her parasol to see whether or not Carson had noticed her. He hadn't, not yet. But they were drawing nearer to him now, they were hardly three yards away from him, and then miraculously, they were passing him.

Sarah fought the urge to look back over her shoulder. She might have been imagining it, but she thought she felt eyes scraping the back of her neck as she passed.

Her other sisters could hardly fail to notice that something was going on. "What on Earth was that all about?" whispered Noelle, drawing back so that she could fall into step beside Sarah.

"Not here," hissed Sarah. She chanced a half-glance over her shoulder. Carson Williamson was several yards away from them now, but as she looked back, she saw his eyes flick onto her. He took a step in her direction, a dawning look of comprehension flooding over his features, but just then, a group of laughing, raucous gentleman swooped between them, plainly intent on nothing more than to bring themselves nearer to Miss Carlisle.

Sarah didn't much like the woman, but she couldn't help but be grateful for the distraction she was providing.

Sarah spun away, then she picked up her skirts and dodged around each of her sisters. Quick as a flash, she flew up the steps of a nearby dock and vanished out of sight. Her sisters squabbled, squeaked and then regained control of themselves as Carson Williamson jogged around the group of men and approached them.

Sarah crouched, out of sight, listening hard as gulls flapped around her over her head.

"Excuse me, ladies. Wasn't there a fourth among you?" she heard Carson's deep voice ask as he neared them.

Always the quickest on the uptake, it was Dianna who responded: "Four of us, sir? We are but three." Sarah could hear the smile in her sister's voice and knew what her face would look like if she could see it. She would be wearing her gentle, flirtatious smile. The one that had driven many a man to pursue a courtship with her.

Sarah felt a flash of anger heat her cheeks, although she couldn't be sure why.

"It was only the three of you...?"

"Yes, sir. Perhaps you should join us in the hotel lounge for a drink of water. The heat of the day appears to be playing tricks on your eyes."

Sarah frowned. Don't invite him to sit down with you, Di. What on Earth am I supposed to do with myself then?

But she heard Carson respond before she had finished her thought. "No, no. I thank you. Please excuse my interruption."

Sarah peered over the side of the dock and watched as Carson strolled away from her sisters, rubbing the back of his head in an embarrassed sort of way. One by one, her sisters turned their eyes up to her. Sarah gulped. Noelle looked excited, Dianna: quizzical, but Charlotte looked as though she would very much like to thump her.

They descended on her with more ferocity than the ocean waves that crashed against the shoreline.

"Who is he?" asked Charlotte immediately, taking hold of Sarah's hand and tugging her down a sandy trail that lead to the boardwalk.

Before Sarah could answer, Noelle was poking her hard in the ribs. "Why were you hiding from him?" she demanded. "He was so handsome!"

"It's not a question of how handsome the man is," said Charlotte, squinting over at Noelle with disapproval. "Has he done something improper?" she whispered conspiratorially. "You looked utterly terrified when you saw him."

"Not... I..." Sarah was grappling for a response.

"Enough, girls," said Dianna. She reached between Noelle and Charlotte and extracted Sarah from between them, silencing their protests with a practiced glare.

"We were talking about it last night before bed," she said. "I'm sorry that I let you get away without telling me the rest of your story," she looked rather cross with herself.

Sarah sighed. Dianna wove down the path between the dunes and led her to a stone bench sitting a few feet away.

"Now," she said, sitting down and pulling Sarah down beside her. "Tell me what happened."

All three of her sisters listened raptly as she told them her story. When she reached the part about slipping over the ledge, Charlotte and Noelle gasped, and Dianna looked very strained.

"But he grabbed me," said Sarah with a shrug. She rubbed absently at the sore spot on her ribs. "He pulled me back up."

"Well," said Dianna, clasping Sarah's hand in both of her own. "Thank heavens for that!"

"It was his fault," insisted Sarah dryly. "I wouldn't have fallen at all if he hadn't–."

"I can't believe you went poking around an old pile of rocks," said Charlotte, scowling. "What would you have done if it had given way and crushed you?"

"Obviously, 'Lotte," said Sarah, still with that dry undertone, "I'd be dead."

Charlotte threw her hands up in the air in exasperation.

"It sounds like a beautiful place," said Noelle. A dreamy look had slid onto her face. "I'd love to see it."

"Absolutely not," said Charlotte stubbornly, stamping her foot as though to get her point across. "It's bad enough that Sarah trespassed there the handful of times that she did without the four of us traipsing off to do it all over again. No. You're not going," she said to Noelle. "And Sarah is never going to go back."

"I don't understand, Sarah," said Dianna quietly. She'd been silent for several moments. "He terrified you, then he saved you, but why did you feel the need to hide from him?"

Sarah growled deep in her throat. "Right. Well, once he had pulled me back in through the window, he decided that I must be suicidal."

Noelle snorted. Dianna, lifted her hand to conceal a small smile. Even Charlotte let out a quiet chuckle.

"I take it you weren't able to dissuade him of this opinion?" Dianna inquired, still trying not to grin.

Sarah scowled at her. "He wanted to take me to the police," she said sourly.

"Oh, Sarah, why didn't you just go with him?" sighed Charlotte.

"What? And have the whole of Manhattan thinking me unstable? Rumors would be flying for decades. Mother would have a stroke. Not a chance," she said, shaking her head.

"What did you do to him?" asked Noelle. Her eyes had gone wide, and she'd sunk into a crouch in front of the bench.

"Nothing he didn't deserve," responded Sarah, bristling.

"Hmm, well, I take it you didn't stop to consider the thought that he might turn out to be someone with whom you may have to rub elbows?" said Dianna plucking at a seam in her gloves. "There's every chance you're going to have to apologize to him at some point."

"No, I will not," growled Sarah. She stood. "If anyone is going to be apologizing, it will be him."

CHAPTER THREE

CARSON

What had he been thinking of? Carson stumbled away from the three elegantly dressed ladies, his mind jumbled and confused. Perhaps the heat of the day was getting to him after all? But no... he glanced back over his shoulder. The three women were still watching him interestedly, whispering to one another.

They were some of the prettiest, and classiest he had yet seen in America. Much unlike the lewd woman on the Southern end of the beach whose clothes seemed to be falling right off her body.

But he had been so sure, for a moment, that he had seen her there amongst them. Peering coyly out at him from beneath one of the lacy parasols. The woman from his ancestor's house. The one who had attempted to throw her beautiful self from the ramparts.

He still couldn't believe it. She had been so lovely, sitting there all on her own, with the light of the setting sun illuminating streaks of red and blonde in her brown hair. He'd thought for a moment that he had stumbled upon some long-forgotten ghost of the waves. Or perhaps a siren. But she hadn't been singing. She had just been sitting there, so dangerously close to the edge. Then she had stood, and something in his heart had told him that she was preparing to leap.

He couldn't imagine a situation arising in which a woman such as she would be so far lost, and in that split second between the moment he had first laid eyes on her and the moment he had realized what she was going to do, he knew he couldn't imagine a world without her in it.

But she was not well, obviously. She needed help. Quite apart from the fact that she had attempted to end her life, her mercurial moods after the fact had solidified the idea in his mind. First, she had been defiant and angry, then quite suddenly, she had been amiable, and then—even more suddenly—she had become interested in him. Were it not for the dark bruise on his shin, he would have thought he had imagined her.

When she had fled, he had tried to give chase, only to find she had vanished from sight. Her horse had been an incredible animal, just as incredible as its rider. Carson hadn't even been able to draw breath before the beast had whipped around the decaying towers of stone and whisked her out of sight.

He sighed, pulled off his hat, and ran a hand through his hair as the coastal breeze whirled around him. Fine grains of sand skittered around his ankles and Carson attempted to smile at two young children sitting a few feet away from him with sand crusting their fingers and toes. They were staring at him with wide eyes, and Carson wondered if he looked a little mad himself.

"Williamson! Oi! Williamson!"

It was a few seconds before Carson recognized the sound of his surname floating to him on the air. He turned to see a broad, barrel-chested man approaching him with a cigar and a smile. He wore a boulder hat atop thin brown curls, and his cheeks were rosy with the exertion of his walk.

"James Sutton, you old dog," laughed Carson as his friend approached him on wide, stockinged feet. "What have you done to your shoes?"

Sutton laughed. "I've left them with my wife. Come and join us?"

Carson looked around. "I was supposed to meet a bank representative at Hotel Brighton in an hour," he said, looking at his watch.

"We can always start a little early, don't you think?" Sutton raised his eyebrows.

"You're the representative?" asked Carson incredulously. "I thought you were a lawyer for the Downbridge firm."

"Use to be," said Sutton puffing out his chest, "but Lucille said she weren't interested in marrying me if I didn't get ahold of a steady, honest position. I guess she thought being a lawyer didn't cover it," he laughed again, then reached forward and gripped Carson's shoulder.

Carson returned the gesture. "It's been a long while since Oxford," he said. "I was aiming to look you up tomorrow morning at Downbridge. It's a stroke of luck that the bank sent you."

"Ha!" laughed Carson. "You had a fifty-fifty shot. My partner is Jeffry Davis from Bentley and Skinner. Remember him?"

"Oh, joy," laughed Carson. "You suppose that blighter will ever forgive us for that business in '83?"

"Not a chance. He brings it up every chance he can get."

The men roared with laughter, clutching at one another.

"We'll have to have lunch," said Carson after a moment, settling himself. "You and me and Jeffry."

"I'll tell him," said Sutton. "He'll look forward to it. Now, get over here, I want you to meet my family."

Carson spent several hours with Sutton. He had to admit, it was immeasurably cheering to see a friendly face. He'd been ready to spend the afternoon with a surly stranger who would want haggle with him over his every word. To his absolute pleasure, the business end of things was concluded within an hour.

Sutton's family was a cheerful lot. His wife had a pinched face and a pointed nose, but she smiled so much you would never notice. They had two boisterous little boys who, by the end of the day, were clinging to Carson like small octopuses, and a baby girl hardly older than three months who had her father's rosy cheeks.

It was hard not to feel jealous of Sutton when he pictured the massive, empty manor house he had just purchased a few weeks ago, with its cold, unfeeling walls and gray lackluster spaces. Carson had always wanted children. Always. But through his schooling, and then the years after it, as his father groomed him to take over the business end of the coal mines, he had never managed to make the time to find a wife.

"This is the thing," said Sutton, "you remember your father's old flame? The one he tried to marry before she ran off to America?"

"Samantha... Russel? Was it?"

"Rothschild," Sutton corrected him.

"Vaguely," said Carson slowly. "What's she got to do with anything?" He never thought much about the widowed woman whom his father had once hoped to marry. She was by the by now. That had all happened when he was eight or nine years old.

"Does the name Brittler ring any bells in that handsome head of yours?"

Sutton began to chuckle as Carson's eyes grew wide. "You've got to be joking," he said irritably.

"Nope. Miss Samantha Brittler, now married to Thomas Brittler of Brittler Steel."

"That's annoying," said Carson.

"That's an in, man," whispered Sutton. "Write to your old acquaintance, perhaps you can do business with her husband."

"Brittler owns his own coal mines. What would he want to do with ours?"

"He's looking to expand from what I hear," said Sutton, nodding his head imperiously. "I'd be jumping on that if I were you. Besides," Sutton added, wiggling his eyebrows suggestively. "He has no less than four daughters, ripe for the picking, each one of them."

Carson rolled his eyes as Sutton winked.

Reluctant though he was to extend the hand of friendship to the woman who had shattered his father's heart, Carson was able to recognize sound advice when he heard it. So it was that the next sunny afternoon found him sitting alone on his back porch, tapping a pen against his knee.

He'd written:

Dear Mrs. Brittler, and then scratched it out. He didn't want to sound as though he was too concerned about her status as Mr. Brittler's wife. *Miss Rothschild,* he wrote, but then he scratched that out too. It would be odd to adress the woman by her maiden name. How in the world was he supposed to go about writing a note like this? *Simply,* he thought. *Do it simply.* He took a breath, then bent his head and began to write.

Mrs. Brittler,

It has been a terribly long time since we were acquainted, but I find myself alone in New York and seeking a

guide that might help me navigate this unfamiliar terri-
tory. With you and your husband's permission, I would be
delighted to call on you anytime, as I have recently taken up
a permanent residence in Brooklyn.

Best,

Mr. Fredrick Carson Williamson

There, thought Carson. Simple. No awkward insinua-
tions. He sat back and gazed around his dreary surroundings. The house he had purchased had lain abandoned
for several years, even though it had once belonged to his
family. His grandfather had sold the property when Carson's great grandfather had passed on, and there hadn't
been a Williamson living in it since that time. Evidently,
the owners had let the land fall to the bank, who had done
very little with it until Carson came along and purchased
it back. The property had housed generations of his family, and he had to confess, he was rather sentimental about
it.

Even the ruin that sat along the cliffs had once belonged to Nicholas Peter Williamson, a wealthy man who
had sailed from England in 1731 and set his roots along
the coast of New York. Now, Carson envied him. In his
time, almost two hundred years ago, Nicholas Williamson
had been surrounded by a populace that consisted of just

over two thousand people. Now, the streets of Brooklyn thronged with more than half a million.

It was a smelly, crowded place, and Carson couldn't help but think that this was not what his ancestor had intended for them. The property was but a few acres long now, having been sold off in bits and pieces by desperate Williamson's as they fell into debt. It ran from the front of the house, which sat up against a busy Brooklyn side street, to the cliffs through the trees behind it. Even with the entire house between himself and the bustle of the city, he could still hear it. Cries of welcome and the jangling and clopping of passing carts and carriages nearly drowned out the sounds from the ocean beyond the cliffs.

Carson stood and stretched. He missed England. There, at least, he had been the owner of a grand estate, not a crumbling gray mass of tasteless brick. But his father had insisted, and so, here he was. In a city so stuffed with people, he could have handed his neighbor a few spare sugar cubes through the sitting room window.

Well, perhaps that was a bit of an exaggeration. His nearest neighbors were blocked from sight by a line of tall trees on either side of the spacious yard. He had a lovely side garden, and it was nice to be able to ride out to the back of his property and view the waves.

He would probably never know why the ruined mansion on the cliffs hadn't been destroyed when the new house was built, or even years afterward. Perhaps the former owners, whether Williamson or not, had been able to cherish the history of the place. Perhaps they had just never gotten around to it.

"Sir? Mr. Williamson?"

Carson jumped, he had been staring idly toward ruin, running his thumb over his lower lip. "Yes, Lee. What is it?"

"You've received a note," said his new butler, his voice rather weak, as though he expected a reprimand for interrupting Carson's thoughts. "From a..." he glanced at the envelope. "A Mr. Sutton."

"Right, well, bring it here then," he said gruffly, holding out his hand. His butler from England had been very reluctant to leave his home, a fact that was a continuous source of annoyance to Carson. He loathed training new people.

The man scuttled toward him, offered him a clumsy bow and back away again. "Lee, come back here a moment," said Carson, watching him.

His butler looked petrified. Carson couldn't fathom what he might have done to inflict this terrifying impression on him. "Lee, I really need you to relax," he smiled grimly at the man, who was several years his senior. "Your job is not in danger and you've yet to give me a reason to disapprove of the way you are organizing my household. Chin up, man. I'm not an employer that you need to be fearful of."

Lee's shoulder sank rapidly. Where they had appeared to be coming out his ears, they now relaxed into a semi-normal position.

"Thank you, sir," muttered Lee.

"Is this your first position as a butler, Lee?" asked Carson, doing his best to hide his exasperation. He's specifically told his father to hire someone seasoned.

"Yes, it is, sir."

Carson sighed. "And before this you were?"

"A footman, sir. A footman at the Devons' up the way." Lee gestured vaguely to his left.

"I see. Very good, Lee. Where are the workers today?"

"In the sitting room and the dining room, sir. They say they'll be finishing up with those rooms today, and with your permission, they'd like to start on the stairway and possibly the upstairs bedrooms."

Carson nodded. "Thank you, Lee."

The butler departed. Carson sat back in his chair. He'd began renovations on the house as soon as he had arrived, starting with his own rooms, of course. The rest of the house was in complete disarray. He'd thought about staying in a hotel, but he decided he'd rather be on the spot in case the workers had any questions for him.

He was regretting this decision very much. He fought the urge to plug his ears as the workers resumed their hammering, having finished with their fifteen-minute break. Grumbling audibly, Carson reached for his letter opener and slit open the envelope from Sutton.

Williamson,

Meet me at the racetrack at One O'clock?

-James Sutton

Carson glanced at his watch, then gave a small yelp. "Lee?!" he shouted into the house. "Have my horse brought around!"

Chapter Four

SARAH

She was growing restless. Saturday was drawing nearer, it was less than a week away, and there hadn't been a single word from her father that suggested she might be allowed to accompany Averleigh to her first race of the season. She knew better than to bring it up with him.

"What did he say? When you spoke to him, Di? How did he react?"

Dianna rolled her eyes. "I told you. He didn't do much of anything besides grunt, frown, and roll his eyes."

"He didn't actually say anything? What did you say to him?"

"I merely pointed out how much of a disappointment it would be for you to miss it. Averleigh does so well on the track. It would be a rather horrid punishment."

Sarah sighed and returned to her pacing. "He hasn't allowed me anywhere near the stables all week," she said. "I haven't even been allowed to attend to her feedings in the morning."

"I'm sorry," said Dianna, although her face said quite plainly: "well, you were rather irresponsible."

Her disapproval of Sarah-Jane's punishment seemed to have lessened slightly after she had discovered the full contents of the story.

"Well, here's something that might cheer you up!" The girls' mother sashayed into the room with a broad grin on her face. Samantha was clothed today in soft, blue muslin. Her skirts rustled as she moved gracefully across the room, ever conscious of her posture.

"I'm going to arrange for you all to meet the son of an...old friend of mine. He's in town on business."

Sarah perked up. It would be a nice to have something to look forward to. "When?"

"I'm going to ask him around for lunch on Thursday," she said, happily.

Sarah narrowed her eyes, suddenly suspicious. Often, any man that her mother approved of this heartily had a large bank account and a wart on his nose. "What's he like?"

"I don't really know," said Samantha. She sank down at the writing desk in the corner of the parlor and began searching for a pen. "I knew him a long time ago," she said with a fond smile on her lips. "He was a very sweet little boy, then."

"How long ago?" asked Dianna. She didn't seem near as interested as Sarah was. She hadn't looked up from her book. "Oh, well, he'll be...twenty-six now? He was only eight years old when I knew him." Their mother located her pen and set about scrolling a note on one of her blue, ribbon-clad invitations.

"How do you know him?"

"As I said, his father and I were old friends." Sarah saw two pink patches appear high in her mother cheeks.

"Who's his father?"

"Enough questions," snapped Samantha, waving her hand, "allow me to finish this up so I can get it sent off."

Sarah caught Dianna's eye, and then both hid their grins in fingers.

Thursday was their first rainy day in weeks. The summer sunshine had been persistent up until then, and Sarah couldn't help but wish the good weather could have held out just a bit longer so that they could have spent the evening in the cottage garden. She had Alice help her don a gown of white lace, hoping it would serve to chase away the gloom. It was a particular favorite of hers in the summertime. She thought it made her hair color settle into one variation of blondish brown.

Her hair was a cacophony of colors. In the winter, without the exposure to sunlight, it darkened to a lank, dirty brown. In the summer, however, it lightened considerably, making her look a pretty, reddish blonde, and in the salty coastal air, it curled as it never did at home. Her nose was straight, and her cheeks were high in her slender face. She looked a lot like their mother. Slender, and petite and very freckly. Her sisters looked very much like their father. At least, Dianna and Noelle did. While Charlotte, with her brilliant red hair, was a different being entirely. However, when the four of them strolled down the street, it was impossible to mistake them as anything other than sisters.

"There you are, miss," said Alice, bobbing Sarah a little curtsy as she gathered her discarded clothes into her arms. "Will you be needing anything else, or shall I go help Miss Noelle dress?"

"No, I'm alright. Thank you so much, Alice."

Her maid smiled and trotted out of the room, leaving the door open behind her.

Sarah turned on her vanity stool to examine her reflection critically. Her hair, still damp from her bath, hung about her face in dark strings. A familiar prick of irritation caused her brow to furrow. She should have asked Alice to stay and help her for another moment. She'd never be able to manage this mess on her own.

"Almost ready?" It was Dianna's voice. She looked very lovely as she stepped through the still-open doorway in a dress patterned with yellow pinstripes, her smile resigned as if she were readying herself for battle. The floorboards creaked beneath her feet as she glided across the room to stand beside Sarah. Her eyes skated over the lank strands of hair that draped around her sister's cheeks. She made a face. "Want me to do up your hair?"

"Yes, please," Sarah almost begged.

Dianna could work miracles on the top of Sarah's head that she never seemed able to manage on her own.

Ten minutes later, her elder sister slid a final pin in place and stood back.

"How's that?" she asked.

"It's perfect, Di. Thank you."

Dianna had somehow managed to twist half of Sarah's hair up onto the top of her head so that the other half cascaded down in riotous curls.

"I don't know what I'd do without you," she said fondly, squeezing her sisters fingers. "You'll have to come over to my house every Sunday when we're both married, otherwise, I'll look like the head of a broom on a daily basis."

Dianna smiled indulgently. "You'll have to learn to manage eventually," she said, and for some strange reason, she looked a little bit sad as she said it. "Still," she said briskly, her expression clearing. "That time is a long way off, yet. Let's head out."

Noelle and Charlotte joined them in the hall. "Ready?" they asked.

"Ready," Sarah echoed. They smiled at one another and then, as one, headed down the darkened hall.

Samantha Brittler was alone in the parlor when Sarah shoved open the door a minute later.

"There you are, at last," she said, looking annoyed. "It's about time. Get settled in, he'll be here any minute!"

"You haven't even told us who it is that we're supposed to be meeting, Mother," said Dianna. She entered the room behind Sarah, meeting their mother's flustered gaze with a scowl of her own.

With a jolt, Sarah realized how very exhausting this all must be for her. Dianna was ten years her senior. She'd gone through this process hundreds of times over with her head held high. After curtsying and interrogating—for that was very much the best word to describe Dianna's approach to courtships— nearly every available gentleman her mother presented, it was clear she had decided that greeting potential suitors was a complete and utter waste of time.

"Can't you at least attempt to treat him kindly, whoever he is?" muttered Sarah under her breath as all four of the Brittler Sisters took seats around the coffee table.

"If he's someone Mother's fond of, I doubt he'll be quite to any of our tastes," growled Dianna. She perched herself rigidly on the ended of the settee and frowned into the small fire dancing in the grate. "It's stifling in here," she said after a moment. "Is there really a need for a fire, Mother?"

Samantha Brittler waved her hand distractedly, peering out the window toward the front garden. "I thought it might bring some cheer into the room," she said with a hint of reproach in her voice. "Do with it what you will. Where has your father got to?" She glanced at the clock on the mantelpiece. "It's half past two. If he doesn't hurry, he'll miss him."

"Do you really think your guest will arrive a half an hour early?" asked Charlotte skeptically.

"Well," Samantha hedged, "he was always very prompt—."

"You mean when you knew him as a child?" interrupted Dianna.

Their mother's cheeks reddened. "I—well... When I say I knew him... It was really more his father that I—."

"What is it you're not telling us, Mother?" asked Noelle, whose eyes had flared bright at the hint of a mystery.

"Nothing," snapped Samantha. She stood, brushing imaginary dirt off of her skirts. "I'm going to check on your father," she said briskly, and she sidled out of the room.

Noelle slumped back in her seat. "Doesn't anything romantic ever happen in this family?" she asked dejectedly, to no one in particular.

Charlotte and Dianna exchanged looks. "I'm completely content with whatever past Mother might or might not have had with this man's father staying shut behind closed doors, thank you very much," said Charlotte scathingly. She walked over to the sideboard and began to pour herself some tea. "Would anyone else like—?" she broke off as she turned away from the window.

Sarah was watching Charlotte's profile, and so it took her a moment to understand what had happened. Charlotte had frozen. The teacup slipped out of her sister's fingers. There was a small tinkling as it shattered on the hardwood floor, and she looked around at Sarah with something akin to panic in her eyes.

"Lottie?!" cried Noelle, leaping to her feet. "Are you alright?"

"Sarah," she hissed. "Sarah, it's him."

"Who?" chorused the girls together.

But just then, there came a knock on the front door. The steady sound of a heavy fist on hardwood echoed dismally through the house, and Sarah realized what Charlotte had meant. There could surely be only one "him" that could instill such a look of abstract horror on her sister's face.

"It's not."

"It can't be."

"We mustn't let him in!"

Charlotte was frozen in place. Noelle and Dianna had both leapt to their feet. Sarah was staring toward the door that led out into the hall. Her mind had gone blank.

"Sarah." Dianna was shaking her arm. "You have to get out of here."

Sarah took a breath and the cogs in her head ground back into action. She felt her knees give a slight tremble as she listened to the sound of the front door opening. Her footing slid a little so that she had to grab the back of the nearest chair for support.

She darted terrified glances around the room, looking for a way out, but the only means of escape was into the hall, from which she could already make out the deep baritone of Carson Williamson's voice emanating.

"I was honored to receive your invitation, Mrs. Brittler. Once I heard you were nearby, I knew I had to reach out."

"I'm so pleased that you did, Mr. Williamson. So very pleased." Samantha Brittler's voice had gone high and breathy.

"He's coming in," said Sarah swiftly. "There's no avoiding it now. Everyone sit down. Look casual."

The Brittler girls scattered like billiard balls. Charlotte stooped to retrieve the shattered remnants of her teacup and shoved it all unceremoniously into a cloth napkin.

Sarah and Noelle collided as they attempted to arrange themselves in the same armchair. A silent battle ensued as the girls fought over the chair. Sarah fell off the cushion onto the rug and her skirts fell into a tangled mess. She leapt up again and just made it across the room to the side table as the door handle turned. She turned her back on the room and busied herself with pouring a cup of tea, trying to ignore the way her hands were shaking.

"I do think so," said Dianna, who had planted herself on the edge of the settee once more and she heard Charlotte give a high, false laugh.

"Girls?" It was their mother's voice. "Girls, this is Mr. Fredrick Williamson."

"Carson, please, Mrs. Brittler. It all gets so confusing when people shout my father's name to get my attention."

Sarah took a deep breath and turned to face the room.

Carson Williamson was standing beside their mother, whose face was shining as she gazed at Carson with undisguised excitement.

He looked wholly detached and rather aloof. His expression reminded Sarah of the one her father wore whenever he was heading into town for business. He didn't fool her for a moment. This wasn't merely a social call, Carson had something to gain by being here. His dark eyes scanned the room with genial approval as he acknowledged each of the Brittler girls with a swift nod. His hair was dark and neat, and stubbornly tidy. He still gave every appearance of a proud captain at the helm of his ship.

"Ladies," he said, with absolutely no hint of embarrassment at having just been ushered into a room where he was outnumbered five to one by women. He looked cocky and self-assured. Clearly, he was comfortable in his skin.

She watched his gaze spin on to each of her sisters in turn, and she had the impression that he was judging them, measuring them up to some invisible standard he held in his mind's eye. And then his eyes found Sarah, and she could pinpoint the exact moment that he recognized her. It took him a single, loud tick of the clock on the mantle, a spare second of gazing into her face before he registered why she was familiar to him.

Carson's handsome, square jaw went slack with shock and his eyes grew wide. Sarah waited for the blow to fall. The clock on the mantle gave another earth-shaking tick.

Then, suddenly, with an abrupt return to his collected state, he looked away. She felt his gaze slide from her as though a dark shadow had passed across her grave, and the air was lightened. She could breathe again.

"Won't you introduce your daughters to me, Mrs. Brittler?" he asked, with every appearance of polite curiosity. His dazzling smile had returned. Had she imagined it? Had he not recognized her after all? It had been very dark in the ruins... perhaps, with a little luck...

"Of course," their mother was all of a flutter. Sarah couldn't remember ever seeing her like this before. As a general rule, Samantha Brittler strove to make an excellent impression on any of her daughters' potential suitors, but this...? Samantha's cheeks were pink as she skipped across the room to Charlotte, whom she clearly thought would make the best impression on Carson.

Charlotte, with her flame-red hair and voluptuous figure, was easily the most attractive of the four sisters. Although Noelle, who was a mere seventeen years, was already a close runner up. That's not to say Dianna and Sarah-Jane weren't pretty. They were, but in a sweeter, simpler way. They were both lean and lithe, with a hint of grace about the way they moved that Noelle and Charlotte never did quite manage to convey.

"This is Charlotte," beamed Samantha, taking Charlotte's shoulder and practically forcing her into Carson's arms.

Carson took a measured step back, but his smile stayed perfectly fixed on his handsome face. "Charlotte," he said, bowing over her hand. Sarah watched the lines around

Charlotte's eyes tighten, but she smiled graciously before withdrawing her fingers from his.

"And this is Dianna, Sarah-Jane, and Noelle."

Carson inclined his head at each of them, his eyes lingering on Sarah.

"Sarah-Jane?"

She swallowed past the lump that had risen in her throat and met Carson's eyes with a smooth indifference. "A pleasure to meet you, Mr. Williamson," she said, bowing her head.

"You remind me of someone," he murmured, running a long finger over his lips in thought, and although he was still several feet away from her, Sarah thought she sensed amusement in his tone.

"Oh, really? I hope it is not a memory of anyone too horrible."

The tension in the room seemed to increase. Noelle let out a high-pitched giggle. Sarah saw Dianna cast her a reproving look behind Carson's back.

Carson's smile broadened. "Unfortunately," he said, and he moved across the room toward her. "I cannot say that the memory that comes to mind is a pleasant one. I can only hope," Carson held out his hand expectantly and Sarah had no choice but to place her fingers into his palm.

"That you will be able to *manufacture* a more pleasant one for me to dwell upon." He planted a soft kiss over her knuckles, and Sarah felt the threat that echoed in his words.

Sarah's eyes narrowed dangerously. "I can assure you," she responded in clipped tones, "that I will do my very best."

CHAPTER FIVE

CARSON

His breath caught, and he gave a small cough. "Forgive me," he said, straightening. He turned away from Sarah-Jane's determined expression of feigned innocence and withdrew a cloth from his pocket. With his face averted, he faked a small fit into his kerchief.

"Could I trouble you for a glass of water?" he said to Mrs. Brittler.

"Of course," she fluttered her hands in her nervous way and proceeded to the side table.

A few moments later, with a glass of water in his hand and the Brittler women bearing down on him, Carson regained his composure once more. He couldn't believe she was here. He'd been combing the streets, looking into the eyes of every beggar and seamstress that he passed, and all the while, his mystery woman had been trotting around in finely wrought gowns, sipping tea and sitting down to dinner with one of the wealthiest families in all of Manhattan.

He cleared his throat, and avoided looking in her direction for a moment, but he couldn't seem to help himself. His eyes were drawn to her.

That night, in the ruins of his family's ancestral mansion, she had looked ghostly. Pale and beautiful, he had become half-convinced he had dreamed her up. Now she stood before him. As solid and as vividly present as he was, and his eyes flicked to her so often he worried he appeared to have a twitch. None of the Brittlers, apart from Sarah, appeared to notice anything strange in his behavior, however, and she was putting on a remarkable show.

If her eyes had not met his with such a vindictive fire, he would think she hadn't recognized him at all. Her sisters were amiable, and chatty. They filled the awkward silence of the parlor with meaningless talk about this thing or that. Carson found this helpful as he recovered from his shock.

He was still watching Sarah. He waited. Surely she would crack before he did. Her behavior in the ruins that night proved she was highly unstable. Did her family know? How could they not?

"Miss Sarah-Jane?" he said her name before he could stop himself. She turned to him slowly, her expression one of mild indignation, and Carson realized he had interrupted the girls' mother. He nodded at her. "My apologies, Mrs. Brittler. I'd didn't intend to intervene, but you said something about the horse races? Down on Brighton Beach?"

All of the women were watching him curiously. "Yes," responded Samantha with a tight-lipped smile. "Yes, Sarah's horse, Averleigh, will be racing this next weekend."

Carson turned back to Sarah. "You'll be riding in the race?" he asked astounded, looking from Sarah to her mother in high astonishment.

Sarah let out a sarcastic laugh. "Of course I won't," she said. She sounded almost angry. "What gave you that ridiculous impression?"

"She's your horse, isn't she?" said Carson, grumpy at having misconstrued her mother's meaning. He reached for his glass of water.

"Yes, but we have a rider, of course," Mrs. Brittler had raised her eyebrows at Carson. "Really. A woman riding in a horse race. How preposterous." She let out a little friendly chuckle and sipped at her tea.

Carson's glanced back at Sarah. Her eyes had narrowed dangerously, and she appeared to be chewing her tongue, as though she were biting back the torrential diatribe she longed to throw at him.

"Tell us about your work, Mr. Williamson," said Mrs. Brittler.

"Carson, please, miss," he corrected her with a smile. His neck had flushed with embarrassment and he was thankful to have a reason to pull his eyes from Sarah. "And truthfully, it isn't very exciting. I—." Carson broke off as the parlor door opened, and a man stepped into the room. He recognized him at once. Even in London, Thomas Brittler often made the newspapers.

He restrained himself from leaping to his feet with difficulty. He felt he ought to spring into a salute. Thomas Brittler was one of *the* most affluential men in all of New York. His business practices were marking the way for millions of others behind him, and that included Carson's father's company. If he could remain on good terms with the man...

Carson made a concentrated effort to relax and stood. "Mr. Brittler," he said in greeting, stretching out his hand.

"Ah, Mr. Williamson, is it? Please forgive my lateness, I was caught up in some paperwork and I didn't hear you arrive."

"Not at all, sir. Not at all." Carson was smiling so widely he thought his face might shatter.

"So," said Mr. Brittler, gesturing for Carson to resume his seat. "My wife tells me she and your father are old friends."

Carson felt his stomach plummet as he sank back onto the cushion. He glanced at Mrs. Brittler, who was determinedly avoiding his gaze. "Yes, that's right," he said uncertainly.

Thomas Brittler looked utterly unconcerned. He gave a sharp nod, and then strolled to the sideboard to pour himself a glass of water. Carson took a hasty sip from his cup.

"So," said Thomas, once he had settled himself down in the only vacant chair. "What brings you to New York, Mr. Williamson?"

Carson watched Thomas's eyes flicker to each of his daughters in a resigned sort of way, and he realized that Thomas assumed he was here to court one of them. He smiled, and his eyes jumped to Sarah-Jane of their own accord.

"I'm afraid I'm here on business," he said.

"Naturally, naturally," said Thomas. He already sounded a bit bored. Carson could feel the man's attention wavering. "Your family is in the coal business, am I correct?"

"Y-yes..." replied Carson slowly, "but I must confess I'm here for rather selfish reasons of my own."

Thomas appeared to sit up a little straighter. "Is that so?"

"It was my father's suggestion that I come," said Carson, and his fingers began to drum on the arm of the settee as he wondered whether or not it was intelligent to bring this subject up so soon after their first meeting, "but I was rather eager to take up the position. We have strong family roots in this area, you see. And there are a few private ventures I wanted to attend to as well."

"Private ventures?" queried Thomas.

The women around the room had fallen unnaturally silent. Carson could sense Sarah's tension in the jerk of her movements, and in the shortness of her breath. She was a mere few feet away from him. He could have reached out and touched her. As suddenly as this thought occurred to him, Carson felt his palm begin to itch. What was wrong with him?

"Private ventures, yes," he responded to Thomas, taking another sip of his water. His cup was empty. He set it down on the little table next to the settee.

"Do you care to elaborate?"

"I-" Carson cleared his throat. "I find myself in need of a wife, sir."

For the first time, Thomas smiled. "A straight forward man," he said approvingly. He crossed his ankle over his knee and, looking pleased, glanced around the room at his daughters. "I like that," he said.

Carson smiled. "Quite apart from that rather embarrassing subject," he said, "New York harbors a seemingly endless list of possibilities. I've been working on a side project of mine that I'm hoping will shortly come to fruition."

He had Thomas's full interest now. "Do tell," he said interestedly.

But Carson shook his head. "At the moment, I'm still looking for investors. I'd be happy to tell you more when things have began moving forward."

"Do you like horses?" Thomas asked abruptly.

Carson was a little take aback by the abrupt change of subject. "Yes, I do."

"Wonderful," said Thomas Brittler, as though something had just been settled. "You'll join us at the races this Saturday."

Sarah-Jane's jaw made an audible sound as it popped open in shock. Carson glanced at her, and then he smiled.

"I'd be delighted."

Chapter Six

SARAH

"I'm not going." Sarah folded her arms, staring furiously at her three sisters, all of whom were gathered conspiratorially in her bedroom.

"You certainly are," snapped Dianna.

Her three sisters were, once again, facing her down like a set of angry wolves.

"How can I possibly..?"

"How can you not?!" squeaked Noelle. "He was ogling you like a love sick schoolboy all afternoon."

"Noelle," Sarah sighed, dropping her face into her hands in exasperation. "He was watching for signs of instability. He thinks I am *insane.* Don't you remember?"

Noelle shook her head. "If any man looked at me the way he was looking at you, I don't think I care how insane he thought I was. "

"You'd say that about any man that you thought was handsome," said Charlotte, "there's more to life than good looks, Noelle."

"That is absolutely untrue," laughed Noel, "I'd say that about any man at all."

All three of the Brittler sisters laughed. The tension broke. Sarah walked over to the window and push aside the drapes.

"What are you looking for?" asked Dianna, "it's not as though he's going to come trundling around the corner again, he just left."

"I'm not expecting him to," said Sarah, "he's put me on edge." She allowed the curtain to fall back into place and turned back to her sisters. "This whole ordeal is been highly embarrassing," she said with a sigh. "I still can't believe it happened."

"I can't believe it happened to you either," said Noelle. "It's not as though anything very exciting ever happens to you."

"When is the last time anything exciting ever happened to any of us?" asked Dianna. Sarah looked at her, her sister was looking forlorn and tired, as though her very life was weighing down her shoulders. As though she were exhausted by her mere existence.

"That's very true," said Noelle. She too was looking at Dianna with some concern. Charlotte however was looking toward the doorway.

"This is been a very unusual day," she said with a sigh. She rubbed her fingers irritably against her temples and turned to exit the room. "I think I'll go have a bath."

Dianna's face flickered back to the present. She turned to face Sarah once more. "You have to come to the race. If you don't show, Carson will think you're afraid of him."

"I am a little bit," said Sarah. She sank down onto one the window seat, stretching her legs out in front of her.

"Perhaps he is the one who is in need of medical attention."

Dianna frowned. "I never thought of that, perhaps he does have some sort of latent issues. Why hasn't he sought a meeting with father directly, to tell him what he saw that night?"

"Your guess is as good as mine," said Sarah on yet another sigh. "I suppose you're probably right. I'm going to have to go. I can't lose face now. Not after today." She glanced out the window once more. "I'm glad he's finally left."

"I'm not," grouched Noelle sycophantically. She winked.

Sarah rolled her eyes and left the room after Charlotte.

She made her way slowly to the side door, carefully avoiding the sound of her mother's voice coming from the hallway, and slipped into the mudroom. It had been almost a week since she had visited Averleigh and she was determined that nothing should keep her from her steed today, not even her parent.

She exited the house and slunk past the front window, expecting any second to hear her voice calling her back. When she had made it a few steps away from the house, she broke into a fast jog, and was entering the family's private livery in under five minutes.

The smell of warm sweaty animals, and hay greeted her. It was a welcome scent, a familiar one, it made Sarah feel at home as nothing else did.

"There's my girl," she said, as she sidestepped the few footmen and grooms around the stable with a happy nod. "Feeling alright?"

Averleigh snorted and stuck her velvety nose eagerly into Sarah's palms. Her long tail swished behind her, and her pelt twitched as she warded of flies.

"She's sharp as a tack, this one," said a voice right behind Sarah, and she jumped.

"Oh, hello, Gibson."

"Miss," said the jockey pleasantly, tipping his hat to her. "I was just getting ready to take Averleigh to the track and put her through her paces."

"Were you?" said Sarah excitedly. "Do you mind if I join you?"

"Not at all, Miss!" said Gibson with enthusiasm. "Always nice to have an extra set of eyes. Keeps us sharp. I'm hoping we can shave a few seconds off our time before Saturday. Let me saddle up Hercules over here and we can all ride over together."

Sarah was practically vibrating with excitement. She loved watching Averleigh run. She was a magnificent creature on any given day, but when she ran... she was incredible. Fit for a king.

An hour later, Sarah was situated on the edge of the stands on the track, a stopwatch in her hand.

Gibson began warming Averleigh up slowly, working her muscles, relaxing her. Averleigh skipped and trotted, occasionally throwing her head back as if to say, "Look. Look how good I'm doing. Now, can we get *moving*?"

Gibson laughed whenever she did this. Sarah admired the man's compassion with her horse. He was firm, and yet gentle. He gave Averleigh just enough instruction to lead her, but not so much that she was suffocated under his demands.

As he began lining Averleigh up, he cast a glance in Sarah's direction. "You have that stopwatch ready?"

Sarah waved the watch in her hand, smiling.

"Alright, let's make this one the one that wins us," Gibson said. He reached down and gave Averleigh a pat, whispering something Sarah couldn't hear in her ear. Sarah felt a pang of jealousy. What she wouldn't give to be in his place.

"Ready?" she shouted. Averleigh snorted. Sarah saw Gibson's knees tighten on her flanks. "Go!"

Averleigh leapt forward and she was off, streaking down the track so fast she was little more than a caramel blur on the landscape. Sarah felt her heart swell as she watched her go. She knew her horse. She liked to think she knew her better than anyone. She'd spent days, weeks even, working with her, playing with her, taking her on long races across the coast. *It should be me.*

Sarah dwelled on this depressing thought as Averleigh rounded the first bend, but she knew absolutely nothing could come of it. A woman riding in a horse race, as her mother so rightly said, was preposterous. She would never be admitted.

Her gaze focused on the way Averleigh's lithe muscles flexed as she sped over the Earth, and she felt the sting of tears in her eyes. Pride. Sorrow, and then complete joy filled her as Averleigh rounded the final bend, her nostrils flared.

She glanced at the stop watch. Her mouth went dry. Averleigh crossed the finish line in a whirl of pounding hooves, and Sarah clicked the watch.

"How'd we do?" called Gibson as he and Averleigh trotted to a halt at the other end of the track.

"Twenty-nine and seven!" shouted Sarah. She was watching Averleigh, whose flanks were cover in a thin sheen of sweat. She thought she heard Gibson swear quietly.

"We need to shave off a few more seconds," he said as they approached. "We'll have a few more go arounds and see what we can make of it."

Sarah nodded, leaning against the balustrade. Averleigh stomped her feet agitatedly.

The evening faded around them. Sarah meandered up and down the stands, her eyes on her horse and rider, her heart nearly bursting with jealousy. As the sun slid lower into the sky, Gibson finally brought Averleigh to a halt.

"I think that will do it for the day," he said wryly. "How was the time on that last round?"

"Twenty-seven and two," said Sarah jovially. She skittered down the stairs and then approached the exhausted pair more slowly. "You did so well," she purred at her horse.

"Thank you, ma'am," said Gibson with a laugh. Sarah noticed a fine layer of sweat dotting his forehead.

Sara laughed as well. "Yes, you did very good," she said, beaming at him. "You're amazing with her. It's like she obeys your thoughts."

"If only," laughed Gibson, "it took a fair amount of time for us to get this well coordinated."

Sarah put out her hand to brush the tips of her fingers against Averleigh's nose. Her horse snuffled. "I like to think she knows me as well as she knows you," said Sarah, with a touch of sadness in her voice.

Gibson climbed from Averleigh's back and led her over to a nearby post. "Oh, she knows you, Miss," he said comfortably. Sarah tagged along behind Gibson. When he turned back around, she supposed a glimpse of her envy must have showed on her face, because he glanced from her to her horse and back again, looking rather flummoxed. Then he said: "Aye, you're just a touch upset that it can't be you riding her to glory this weekend."

Shock filter in to Sarah's system. Was she really that transparent? "I…"

"It's not anything to be ashamed of, miss," said Gibson as he removed the bit from Averleigh's mouth. "She's your horse. Makes sense to me that you'd want to ride her."

Sarah felt her shoulder's relax. "I can name a handful of people who would disagree with you," she said, patting Averleigh's flank. "But it's a nice thing to dream about."

"Seems a right shame," said Gibson. He sat down on a bench and removed his cap. "I wouldn't want to see someone else on my horse. Nope. The idea does not interest me at all."

Sarah sat down beside her friend. "I don't much like it either," she said, gazing at Averleigh with misty eyes. "But it really can't be helped, and Averleigh deserves a victory."

"That she does, Miss," said Gibson, "but perhaps you deserve a victory of your own as well."

Sarah thought about that for a moment, her eyebrows pulling together. "What are you suggesting, Gibson?"Gibson gave a chuckle. "I'm only suggesting that, sometimes, the answer to our dreams is hiding just beneath the tip of our nose."

"It isn't possible," said Sarah. "Women can't ride in the race. It would never be allowed."

"Well, perhaps not in this race," muttered Gibson. "We'd have to get you trained up a bit first." He winked, and Sarah's mouth opened in astonishment. "That is, of course. If you're willing."

"Of course, I am!" squealed Sarah, forgetting herself for a moment. "Of course!"

"Well, then," said Gibson, wincing as he inserted a gnarled finger into his ear and rotated it. "We'll have to get you properly outfitted, won't we?"

⚜

Carson

He sat by the empty fireplace, staring into its depths as though he could see the spirit of the flames that had once flickered within it. He held a tall brandy in one hand, and an open book in the other. The book was for show. He glanced at it whenever he heard a member of his household pass by the open doorway that led into the hall. The day was at its end. His workers had gone home, and Carson was feeling himself wilt in the silence.

Before Sarah, he'd reveled in the evening quiet as it encompassed his stark surroundings. Now though, his thoughts took advantage of the silence like a pickpocket takes advantage of a busy street. Sarah's face was flitting in and out of his mind swiftly and silently, leaving traces of honeysuckle in the air around him.

He couldn't seem to stop himself from dwelling on her image, and on the few encounters that he had so far had with her. Why? Why would a privileged woman of such breathtaking beauty seek to end her life? His mind had gone around and around in circles, spinning ropes between the same unanswerable questions. He replayed the scene in the ruins again. Looking for anything that suggested a reason, but to no avail.

With a frustrated sigh, he let the book drop onto his lap and turned his gaze toward the far window across the room. The sky was fading to an inky black outside. The room around him was clothed in shadow.

Sarah was unstable. There. That was a fact. Carson liked dealing with facts.

Her family was evidentially unaware that she was suicidal. At the Brittler's summer cottage this afternoon, he'd detected no sign of tension in any person, save for himself and Sarah. There. That was another fact.

So, all that remained was to decide what to do with the information that was now in his possession. He *could* search out a hospital, and try to discover the proper course of action, according to a medical professional. But no. That wouldn't work. Imagine if they laid hold on Sarah-Jane and carted her away to an asylum. He shuddered. But perhaps that was what was good for her? Even if it was a rather horrible prospect... surely her family would see that it was all for the best. She might leave the hospital completely cured. *Or she might never leave at all.* Carson shuddered again.

He didn't like the idea, but it wasn't his decision. No. It was Sarah's family who would make that call, not him. So, surely, they must be made aware of her condition. It was for them to decide the proper course of action, not him.

Carson sipped at his drink, his opposite hand balled into a tight fist. The unfairness of it all crashed down on him. That such a sweet, pretty thing would be so very mad. Mad enough to end her own life. Well, that was a crime in itself. Perhaps she had some great misery inside of her. Something no one in her world could see. Perhaps she suffered from an unrequited love?

He imagined some rich, pompous suitor who had broken her heart, and anger bubbled up inside of him like hot wax, spilling onto his face so that he found himself gritting his teeth to remain calm. Any man would have to be mad not to love a woman like her.

Chapter Seven

⸺ ❧ ⸺

SARAH

She was perched astride Averleigh, each clip-clopping step making her chin bob in the cool, misty air. Saturday morning had dawned its usual coastal gray haze, and the sun was just beginning to burn color into the day. She was wearing a bright white gown of lace with capped sleeves. It hung down the left side of Averleigh's saddle, dangling over the stone walkways as they passed.

Sarah glared at the back of her father's head as he trotted along on his prized stallion just ahead of her. He had waited until the very last second to inform her that she would indeed be joining them today, and although Sarah knew that she would be allowed to attend the race, she had still not had as much time as she would have liked to get herself ready.

Her scowled deepened as she recalled the main reason for his abrupt change of mind.

"He's clearly very interested in her, Thomas. We can't keep her from going. All the girls will have to attend!" her mother's voice had been very shrill that morning as she tried to conceal her irritation. Mr. Williamson was an extremely eligible suitor, if he was interested in Sarah, then by golly, anywhere he would be was the place to be. At least, according to Mrs. Brittler.

Sarah couldn't fathom why her father had taken such a rapid interest in Mr. Williamson. He'd hardly spared a glance for any of the other available young men their mother had trotted out for them. What was it about Carson that made him so keen?

Behind her, the family carriage jolted over the uneven track that led to the race course. She could hear her mother discoursing loudly on the fact that Sarah had insisted on riding Averleigh.

"There's plenty of room in here with us. Really. What a display."

"You act as though you don't know Sarah at all, Mother," laughed Dianna's voice. "Averleigh is her whole world. Why wouldn't she want to ride her?"

At this, Sarah couldn't help the grimly satisfied expression that crept onto her face. Precisely. Why wouldn't she want to ride Averleigh? To the race. In the race. To victory.

Sarah felt brim-full of confidence in the beast beneath her. Averleigh would win today, with Gibson astride her. And in a few weeks time, after she'd gained some experience, they would win the championship together.

As they neared the stables, Sarah saw that they were by no means, the only people making their way toward the race track. Carts and horses with loudly guffawing gentlemen planted upon their backs, fancy dressed ladies strolling along the path that led from the nearby beachfront hotel. All of them intent on seeing a good race, and many of them approaching the stalls to pick the horse they thought would be the most likely to win. Sarah saw several men, and even a woman or two, clutching betting slips. A few of them held them up to their friends, shouting to be heard over the gathering crowd.

"It's got to be Frolicking Fire, old boy. No doubt about that!"

Sarah grinned. In a few hours time, that older gentlemen would be paying his debts with a sour expression indeed.

She edged Averleigh through the crowd to the much quieter stables, still following her father's lead and waving to her mother and sisters while the carriage trundled away towards the stands.

Averleigh had a stall reserved for her in the farthest corner of the stables. Sarah slid gracefully from her horse's back and led her inside while her father tied his horse to a post.

"There's our champion!" called Gibson when he noticed them approaching. He was stretching, bouncing slightly on the spot, looking excited.

"Gibson," said Thomas, wringing the jockey's hand enthusiastically. "How are you? Feeling well? Confident?"

"A'course!" said Gibson, eyeing Averleigh over Thomas's shoulder. "How's our girl today?"

"Energetic," said Sarah. "She knows what's going on."

"Well, naturally," said Gibson, giving Sarah a friendly wink. "The beasts will talk to ya if you let them."

Sarah giggled. Thomas looked on imperiously, with a fair amount of pride in his eyes.

"Not racing yer old nag this time around?" Gibson asked Thomas. He had just caught sight of Thomas's horse, and his eyes had lit with the enthusiasm of a true horseman.

"He's too old to race today," said Thomas with a smile.

"That old boy? He can't be six years old yet?"

"He'll be ten this Fall," said Thomas.

"No," said Gibson disbelievingly. He hopped toward the stallion, looking as though he had springs attached to the balls of his feet. "Just look at him," he said appreciatively. He must be seventeen hands. Magnificent."

"Thank you," said Thomas, beaming even more widely. "Well, Gibson. If you're alright here, I think I'll go place my bets. Sarah?"

"I'll be along in just a moment, Father. I just want to get Averleigh settled in." Thomas Brittler nodded and strode away from them. "Are we still on for Tuesday afternoon?" Sarah asked Gibson, turning to look at him.

She was half-convinced that he would have already changed his mind. Teaching a woman the tricks of his trade was not an altogether advisable activity.

"Of course, Miss," said Gibson with a smile. "I'll meet you on the track with Averleigh. But make sure to bring the clothes I leant you. We don't want you to be recognizable."

"Yes. I will." Sarah's grin was so broad that her cheeks ached. Together, she and Gibson made their way over to Averleigh's stall. "Be honest," Sarah said when they reached it. "What do you think her chances are."

"I'd say they're very good," whispered Gibson conspiratorially. "She holds one of the fastest times for the quarter mile in the county, and her endurance is next to none. I'd say she has a very good chance of winning today."

"I think so too," whispered Sarah.

"She certainly is a beauty," said a voice just behind them. Sarah whipped her head around so fast that her long hair slapped her cheek.

"Mr. Williamson," she said, acknowledging the man with a glare. "What brings you into the stables? I would have thought you preferred to retain a negligent knowledge of anything that might occur beneath the apparent," growled Sarah, noticing as she did so, how utterly delightful he looked in his crisp suit.

A look of irritation flashed over Carson's handsome face. "I was looking for you," he said, returning her filthy look with interest. "Your father told me you would be here. Might I have a word? In private?"

Sarah looked around for Gibson, her eyes ready to plead that he remain by her side, but the man had mysteriously melted out of sight.

"I have nothing to say to you," Sarah spat at Carson, her eyes flashing in every direction, searching for eavesdroppers. "What are you doing here?"

Carson's look of irritation deepened. "It is as I said. I wish to speak with you."

Sarah crossed her arms in front of her chest. "Is that so?"

"Yes." Carson glanced around. "I believe a conversation concerning the very serious matter of our first meeting is long overdue."

Sarah waited for a moment to see if he was going to elaborate. "Have you come to apologize?" she asked finally.

"Apologize?" Carson sputtered. "What for?!"

"For your horrid assumption of my character and sanity," said Sarah, and her small foot gave a little stamp of its own accord.

"On the contrary," said Carson, "I came here today to confront you."

"Oh?" Sarah made absolutely no attempt to disguise her ire. "Then I am very sorry to inform you that your attempt has been sorely wasted. I've absolutely no wish to lend an ear to your distorted opinion on the matter."

"Distorted? How so?"

Sarah-Jane snorted in disgust. "You are incorrigible. I can't believe that you are still under the impression that I intended to end my life that night. You startled me. I slipped. There is nothing more to it."

"Really?" said Carson, and bizarrely, his face twisted into a look of utmost fury. "Is that a fact?"

"Yes, it is."

"Are you really so determined to convince me of that?"

"Yes, I am!" squawked Sarah, and her little foot stamped at the dirt again, sending up a tiny cloud of dust.

"Then you wouldn't mind if I attached myself to you?"

Confusion flitted into her furious, racing thoughts. "What do you mean?"

"Well," said Carson slowly, and he took another step towards her. "If you were suicidal..."

"Which I am certainly not," interrupted Sarah.

Carson held up his hands, taking a step nearer to her as a jockey and his horse trotted by. "*If* you were suicidal, you shouldn't ever be left on your own. And... if you are not, what better way to prove yourself to me then by spending a bit of extra time with me?"

Sarah thought about this for a moment before deciding to comment. "And how should it look to my family? To our friends?"

"Why... it will look as though I am paying court to you."

Sarah glanced at Averleigh. If Carson was by her side every moment of every day... when would she find time to train for the race with Gibson? She looked at Carson. His face was determined. The expression looked oddly familiar to her. She couldn't place the reason why, but something told her it would be very unwise to attempt to talk him out of this idea. He had made a decision.

"Fine," she said sharply. "I will play the part of your interest, but only to prove to you how very wrong you are about me."

"Then a deal is struck," said Carson, looking pleased for the first time. He held out his arm. "Shall we begin?"

"What? Now?"

"Of course," said Carson, and he beamed as Gibson approached them.

"We're pressed for time, Miss," he said. "We need to get warmed up before the race begins at one o'clock."

"Yes," said Sarah-Jane blankly. "Yes, of course, Gibson. Thank you." She came back to herself a little as she strolled over to Averleigh. "Good luck today, beautiful. Run hard." Averleigh tucked her velvety nose into Sarah's hand, and Sarah placed a gentle kiss between her eyes. "Run hard," she whispered again.

She whirled to face Carson, who still held out his arm to her, obviously waiting for her to take hold. With a sigh, she took a few steps forward and patted Gibson's arm. "Good luck," she said to her friend.

Gibson bobbed his graying head. "Thank you, Miss," he said. "We'll do you proud."

Sarah nodded, feeling her excitement creep up once again, despite the strangeness of the situation she had been thrust in to. She cast Carson a dark look and then took hold of his outstretched arm. "Quickly," she muttered sharply, "My family will be missing me."

"Yes, ma'am," said Carson. He nodded to her, and they strolled off together to find a place in the stands.

As they walked, Sarah tried not to notice Carson. She tried not to feel the solidity of the arm beneath her fingers, or the warm delicious scent of oak and overt masculinity that seemed to emanate from him. She took fast, measured steps in silence, and was utterly relieved when she was allowed to relinquish her grip.

"There you are!" called her mother as Sarah and Carson approached. "We wondered whether you had forgotten the way."

"Not at all, Mother," said Sarah, feigning interest in the large clock on the wall above the commentator's podium. "I was merely giving Mr. Williamson a tour of the stables."

Mrs. Brittler was beaming at them both. "Very good, very good," she said excitedly. "Were you impressed with what you saw, Mr. Williamson?"

"Carson, please, ma'am. And yes, I daresay, this is a very fine establishment."

"Indeed," said Thomas Brittler, chiming in to the conversation unexpectedly. "I quite enjoy the Brighton Beach races every summer, don't I, dear?" he said to his wife.

Mrs. Brittler cast her husband a glowing look. One that she reserved especially for him. "Yes," she said. "He's dragged us here every year since they opened in '79."

Carson was nodding enthusiastically. "I can see why," he said, looking around.

"Have you placed your bets?" asked Thomas. He was examining Carson, as though he was trying to detect him in a lie.

"I'm absolutely wretched at the betting side of things," said Carson amicably. "I emptied my pockets last week on a poor sap that came in dead last."

"Awe. You've just never had a bit of good, sound advice in the area. Come quick, before they close the box." With that, Thomas began to march away, not bothering to look over his shoulder to see whether Carson was following him. Carson grinned, shook his head, and followed.

With that, Thomas began to march away, not bothering to look over his shoulder to see whether or not Carson was following him. Carson grinned, shook his head, and followed.

Sarah's mother was beaming at her. "Well," she said as soon as the two men were out of earshot. "It looks as though Mr. Williamson has set his sights on you, my dear."

"Yes, it appears he has," muttered Sarah, trying not to display her sour mood.

"I think he's absolutely wonderful," Samantha chirped, turning to gaze fondly after his departing back. "A very upstanding gentleman."

"Yes, isn't he?" said Sarah quickly. She was avoiding Dianna's eye. Her sister was gazing at her quizzically. Charlotte and Noelle were looking around the stands, speaking behind their fans to one another.

A loud gong sounded. Sarah stood on her tiptoes to see the jockey's chivying their horses into line on the field.

"It's almost time," she said eagerly.

The Brittler's had a private box in the stands. The view was perfect. She found a seat between Noelle and the edge of the box, inwardly thinking that this way, Carson could not hope to sit by her, but her plan was foiled.

"Sarah, no. Sit up here beside me. Leave some room for Mr. Williamson to sit down beside you," she barked.

"Of course," sighed Sarah. "Heaven forbid that I would like to enjoy the race," she added under her breath, but her mother did not hear her. She was looking around for her husband.

Carson and Thomas reappeared after a few moments, just as the second gong sounded.

"We just caught them," said Thomas happily. "Scooch a bit, my dear, you've hardly left any room at all," he added to Sarah. Sarah glowered at Carson as he sat down, but he returned her venomous look with an easy-going smile that pricked her nerves to even greater heights.

"We're all lined up now! Ladies and gentlemen, please take your seats, the race will begin in three minutes' time. Hold tight to those betting slips!" The commentator had climbed onto his stand and was now shouting into a speaking trumpet as he addressed the crowd.

Sarah shifted eagerly, staring down at the track. She could see Averleigh treading her feet. *Calm her down, Gibson,* she thought. *She needs a decent footing when the gun goes off.*

Two minutes. Every face in the crowd looked excited. Sarah was sizing up the competition, even though she already knew each of the horses' names by heart. She could make out a dappled gray that went by the name of Daggers Point, and a smoky black called Nelson. They would be tough to beat. She'd heard that their times were excellent. There was also a splash white called Gambit, and a black called Liberty Bell. The competition would be fierce.

Sarah could feel her blood pounding in her ears already. One minute to go. Averleigh was still shifting. She wasn't the only one, but Sarah willed her horse to quiet. She needed a good start. She could see Gibson leaning down to pat her, speaking quietly in her ear.

Thirty seconds. Twenty. Ten. Sarah glanced at the clock. Time froze. The gun sounded. The horses exploded away from the starting line and all was thundering chaos as they shot forward as one.

Averleigh took a middle ground, her hooves clattering beside the dappled gray. They were neck and neck, and then Averleigh was rounding the first bend, and she had past him. She was scrambling past the others, her choco-late hooves kicking up clouds of dust. *No, no, Gibson. Don't let her give it her all too early in the game. She still has three more laps to go.* But Averleigh was rounding the final curve now. The horses flashed past the starting line with Gambit in the lead, Averleigh in hot pursuit, Daggers Point on her tail.

Sarah had shot to her feet. She had her hands pressed to her cheeks. The crowd around her was shouting. The women were laughing at the men as they bounded up too. Charlotte was cheering. Noelle was clapping her hands. Thomas Brittler was watching the race with his eyes wide and his brow furrowed in concentration.

The horses shot past the starting line for the third time. This was the final lap; Sarah's insides had turned glacial. Gambit had slowed. Averleigh had slunk up behind him, and they were holding close, the sound of the horses' hooves reverberated through the stands. It was the only thing Sarah could hear.

There was a disturbance. The crowd began to shriek. Nelson had pulled forward along the left side of Gambit. He was overtaking Averleigh. He was shooting forward, and then it was over. In five gut-wrenching, heart-stop-ping seconds Nelson flew over the finish line in first, his rider bent low over his back. Gambit and Averleigh followed, still neck and neck. The flags flashed down.

It took Sarah the space of a moment to realize what had happened. *So close,* she thought despairingly. *She was so close.*

It was as though someone had turned the sound back on. Sarah could hear again. Dianna was pulling on her arm, beaming. "She did so well, Sarah! Did you see? She was fantastic! She must have placed second. She was right behind the black."

"Averleigh, isn't it?" asked Carson in her ear. "She was incredible. I thought she had it."

"Well, I'm sure she placed," said Thomas, who was dabbing at his brow with the sleeve of his suit. "A very close race indeed. Let's go speak to Gibson."

Her father held out his arm for Sarah's and she took it, feeling dazed, and walked down the steps until they came right to the edge of the track, where they hailed Gibson, who was rewarding Averleigh with a long drink from the nearby troughs.

"Very good! You kept right on her. It was perfect. She looked like something from another world."

"She's got the speed," said Gibson. He looked a little sour. "I'm sorry we couldn't scrape first for you today, Miss," he said to Sarah.

"You've nothing at all to be sorry for," she said, her dazed expression breaking into a smile at last. "You were both incredible."

"Thank you. I-," but he was cut off as the Commentator, who'd been convening with the judges, climbed back onto the podium.

"Attention! Ladies and gentlemen! Attention please! I've just been informed of the standings. In first place, we have Nelson a thoroughbred owned by Henry Cook." There were cheers and whistles from the crowd. "In second place," the entire company appeared to hold its collective breath. "We have Gambit of Broomhaven, owned by Mr. Carl Grimsby!" There were cheers and boos. Sarah watched her father wince slightly, she knew that several people had been betting on Averleigh to have ranked higher. Her father included. "In third place," called the commentator, shouting into his speaking trumpet. "We have Averleigh, owned by Ms. Sarah-Jane Brittler!" Heads swiveled in her direction. An echo of cheering went up from the crowd. The commentator went on down the list, but Sarah had stopped listening.

"Not bad at all," she whispered, looking down at Gibson. Very good, in fact."

Gibson shrugged, "We'll have another chance to beat them old dogs, just you wait."

The crowd began to peter out. A few people stopped to congratulate Sarah and her father. While others, with glum expressions, headed toward the gate to pay their dues. Sarah witnessed the older man who had bet on Frolicking Fire glaring at anyone who looked at him. She smiled sadly, and hoped he hadn't lost too much.

"Won't you join us for a late lunch at the hotel Mr. Williamson?" Sarah turned around to see her mother and sisters coming towards them, accompanied by Carson. She groaned inwardly.

Carson seemed to have guessed what she was thinking, or perhaps it was written all over her face, because his cheerful smile widened as he said: "I'd be delighted, Mrs. Brittler, thank you."

Chapter Eight

Carson sat beside Sarah all through the remainder of the afternoon. She flushed each time his hand brushed hers, and tried not to think about the real reason he was there.

She couldn't believe that any man could be so interfering. It was one thing to report a mad woman to the police, or even to inform her parents, but to actually insert yourself in her life? Surely... surely he had some sort of ulterior motive.

Sarah was suspicious, and angry. How on Earth would she ever convince this pig-headed gentleman that she was sane? She couldn't continue to repeat the facts to him, as he was clearly deaf to everything but his own opinions. He was infuriating. And he wouldn't stop touching her!

There it was again, his fingers, lightly brushing over her wrist as he reached for his water glass. She looked at him, trying to judge what he meant by this casual contact, but Carson wasn't looking at her. He was deep in conversation with her father. They were talking about a hotel and something to do with investors.

Her mind latched onto the conversation.

"Of course," Carson was saying as he lifted his glass to his lips, "the venture would have to be completely separate from my father's company. I've no wish to tap into his resources. So, you see my predicament. I have already secured enough on loan from the bank to begin filing permits and purchasing the land, but... investors are a must."

That was it. That was the reason. Carson was going to try and blackmail her father into investing in his scheme! How dare he?! She felt her chest heating. Who did he think he was?!

She glared at him over her untouched meal and bit her tongue. Carson glanced at her. He seemed alarmed by her expression. "Miss Sarah-Jane, are you alright?"

Sarah glanced around the table. Her family was all staring at her. Dianna, who had also been watching Carson speak with a calculating gaze, was looking at her in puzzlement. Sarah raised her eyebrows at them and begin fanning herself with her napkin. "Oh, not at all," she responded curtly. "It must be the heat of the day." She looked across the table at her sister. "Dianna, why don't you take a walk with me?"

"Shall I accompany you?" asked Carson, setting down his knife and fork and looking at her with concern. Sarah repressed a growl. He was a very good actor. How could she deny him without making a fool of herself?

Dianna got to her feet. "I'm sure we'll be alright on our own, Mr. Williamson," she said, arranging her skirts around her ankles.

"I insist," said Carson and he stood too.

Dianna looked affronted. She was not used to being contradicted.

Samantha Brittler cleared her throat, looking meaningfully at her eldest daughter.

"Very well," said Dianna smoothly, adding a brittle smile. "We'll head over the way to the shops and walk along the board-walk, shall we?"

Sarah stood too, and together, the three of them strode away from the table.

"I've found you out," said Sarah sharply to Carson as soon as they rounded the corner of the hotel and were away from prying eyes. "I know your game."

"What game?" said Carson, appearing taken aback.

"You're trying to make it out that I am mad, and then you're going to blackmail my family with the information. I see what you're about Carson Williamson," Sarah poked Carson hard in the chest.

"Don't' be so ridiculous," responded Carson, now on the defense, looking to Dianna, as though hoping for some sort of aid.

Dianna gazed from Sarah to Carson, looking very bemused. "What is this all about?" she asked. "I must admit, I was rather confused by the coziness between the two of you today. Especially after everything that happened in the ruins."

Carson looked at Dianna in high astonishment. "You are aware of that unfortunate business?"

"Of course she is," said Sarah furiously. "I tell Dianna everything. I'm not about to keep something like this a secret now, am I?"

"I just assumed..."

"Let me put your mind at ease, Mr. Williamson," said Dianna matter-of-factly, lowering her voice to a whisper as a couple strode by them arm-in-arm. "Sarah-Jane is not, nor has she ever been, suicidal. I'm not sure what you think you saw that night, but I can assure you that you are mistaken in your impression of my sister."

Carson took a step back from them both. "Well," he said gruffly. "Well, it was… It appeared…" he now looked very uncomfortable. "How was I supposed to have known?" he said at last. "There she was. Right on the edge, looking down into the water, and suddenly…"

"As I *told* you before, Mr. Williamson," said Sarah, doing her utmost to remain calm. "I had no intention of jumping to my death that night. Your sudden appearance startled me and I slipped. There is *nothing* more to it than that."

"Of course," said Carson. He looked very ruffled indeed. "Of course. Well, I… I owe you an enormous apology Miss Sarah. I can only hope that you understand I was acting out of concern for your safety."

"Were you now?" asked Sarah scathingly. "Then what is this business about investors? What are you trying to pull?"

Dianna was watching Carson, her eyes narrowed. Sarah was staring at him too, doing her very best not to notice the way his gray eyes shone in the late afternoon sunlight or the way his chin was perfectly square, as though his face had been carved from marble.

"I'm not trying to pull anything," said Carson. His gray eyes sought Sarah's. "Truly, I am not."

Sarah didn't know why she believed Carson Williamson. Perhaps it was a trick of the light, or the earnest way he was looking directly into her face. She didn't know why she believed he meant her and her family no harm... but she did.

They returned to the table, Sarah feeling much more comfortable in her skin. Having finally convinced Carson that she was as sane as he was, she was finally able to see a bit of humor in the situation. A tiny bit.

The change of circumstances seemed to suit Carson as well. He had relaxed into his chair. For the first time, Sarah was able to view him as a young man, rather than as a threat, and for the first time, she allowed herself to be charmed by him. He really was very good-looking. She remembered how he had looked that night in the ruins. How he had stood, tall and fierce, intent on protecting her from herself, and she had to admire him for his nerve.

She was sure that, in time, she would come to appreciate the way Carson had handled the situation, but for now, Sarah was just glad that the whole business could be brought to an end.

The Tuesday morning following Averleigh's first race was a dull, cloudy gray, and Sarah had a very hard time finding an excuse to remove herself from the rest of her family.

"You can't possibly want to go into town on a day like this," said her mother. "The winds from the sea will give you the chills."

"I really must visit the dress-maker, Mother," said Sarah sternly. "I'm in desperate need of a new gown."

"What for?" asked Noelle through a lazy yawn. Sarah glared at her.

"She's trying to impress Mr. Williamson, of course," laughed Dianna. She gave Sarah a little wink, and Sarah couldn't help but be grateful for her assistance. Mrs. Brittler's expression brightened at once.

"Well," she said, eyeing the frayed hem on the dress Sarah was now wearing. "I suppose a new gown wouldn't hurt. Perhaps Mr. Williamson would be interested in accompanying you to the charity auction next week."

Sarah smiled, but did not respond. Instead she strolled over to her mother, kissed her cheek and said: "I'll be back in a couple of hours."

With the clothes that Gibson had leant her safely stored in her carpet bag, Sarah made her way out to the carriage before her mother could change her mind. Never in her life had Sarah imagined that she would find herself in such a strange situation. This was something she didn't even dare to share with Dianna, an altogether uncomfortable experience. Trying to keep a secret from her elder sister was like trying to keep herself from being sick. The details leaked out of her mouth before she had a chance to call them back, and what she didn't give away... Dianna always guessed. Knowing this, Sarah-Jane had been very careful not to arouse her sister's suspicions. It had been much easier than she thought it would be. Dianna appeared to be very distracted as of late.

After telling the footman to stop on the corner, two or three streets away from the track, Sarah bundled herself into the closed carriage and pulled the shades down on every window.

If she had thought that avoiding her family was the trickiest part of the operation, she was wrong. Changing into a man's clothes inside a moving carriage had to be one of the most uncomfortable experiences of her entire life. With each turn, Sarah lost her balance and was nearly tossed out of the carriage door. She couldn't suppress the embarrassing image of what might happen if she did fall out of the family carriage with her clothes half-off.

At last, after much painstaking effort, she managed it. She pulled on the riding boots, thankful that Gibson was such a tiny man, and began to lace them. Last, but not least, she tucked her hair into the cap he had provided, and then glanced down at her frame. Not a single person that she knew would ever recognize her dressed like this... or, at least, that was what she and Gibson had hoped.

Sarah climbed from the carriage and looked up at her footman. Kincaid glanced down at her and then did a double take. "Miss?" he hissed, looking at her in high astonishment.

Sarah raised a finger to her lips and tossed Kincaid a shining coin. "Not a word, Kincaid. Is that understood?"

"Of course, Miss, but... what on Earth are you doing dressed like that?"

"It's nothing. I'll be back in a couple hours. If anyone asks, you dropped me at the shops, alright?"

Kincaid look doubtful. "Perhaps I should accompany you?"

"No," hissed Sarah. You'll be recognized. I'm not going far, and then I shall have Gibson walk me back."

"Gibson? The jockey? Miss... what are you up to?"

"Never mind. I'll be back in a bit. Thank you, Kincaid."

The footman shrugged. "Suit yourself, Miss. Holler loud if you need me. I'll come running."

"Thank you," said Sarah again, and then she set off. She darted around the carriage, keeping her head down and her shoulders hunched as she moved toward the busier street just ahead of them.

She was sure that no one would look twice at her. She was small of stature, and in these clothes, completely invisible.

She stayed close to the small coastal buildings on either side of the street, breathing in the salty sea air, and reached the next road without any sort of incident, although her heart was pounding so loudly in her chest she thought that it might burst. She glanced up to make sure that she was heading the right way and then ducked her head as a strong breeze rent the still air. She turned left toward the track and felt the wind tearing at her. Suddenly, the cap that Gibson had lent her was ripped from the top of her head. Sarah's dirty blonde hair cascaded around her face, whipping at her cheeks. She snatched at the cap, but the wind stole it from her grasp.

Darting, terrified looks around, lest she be spotted, Sarah lunged after the hat. No one was watching her. No one had seen. No one except...

Her cap landed on the sandy walkway a few feet in front of her and a leather clad foot descended upon it.

Sarah reached out to take it, but someone else already had hold of it. The foot lifted, and the man straightened with the cap in his hands.

"Thank you," Sarah muttered, trying to make her voice grumble like her father's always did. She reached for it once more, but...

"Sarah?"

Sarah gulped and looked up. Carson Williamson looked down at her, his eyes wide. He looked stunned, and more than a little angry.

Without a word, Sarah ripped the cap out of his hands and smashed it onto her head, tucking her hair back inside of it. "Thank you," she said again. Then, without offering Carson a single word of explanation, she dashed away.

"Sarah-Jane!" called Carson after her, but Sarah did not turn around, she did not look back.

Just when he had stopped thinking that she was insane... she had to go and do something like this.

"Sarah! Wait!" Carson was coming after her. She could hear his heavy feet pounded at the path.

"Go away!" she called back to him, and she picked up her pace.

"Sarah! Stop, please!"

She was almost there though. She could see the track now, and she thought she could even make out the petite figure that was Gibson standing beside Averleigh. They were waiting for her to join them. She was going to do this. She was going to... "Oof!!"

Carson had tackled her around the waist and pulled her down to the ground. Sarah looked around wildly for someone to help, but there was no one in sight. The narrow lane that led to the race track was completely deserted.

"Get off 0f me!" shouted Sarah. "Take your hands off of me this instant!"

"No!" Carson shouted the word into Sarah's face and she was so shocked that for a moment, she forgot to struggle. "You are going to tell me what is going on this time! No running. No hiding. What am I supposed to think, Sarah? This is exactly what happened last time. I see you do something completely mad and then you run from me before you bother to explain yourself!"

"Would you listen?!" Sarah shouted back. She was seething. She'd never been so embarrassed in all her life. "Would you listen to a word I said? You didn't listen last time. No. You were quite ready to draw your own conclusions. It didn't matter what I said that night! Now, get off of me!"

"Fine!" yelled Carson, and he released Sarah so suddenly that her arms fell limply to the ground. "Fine," he said a little more calmly, although his eyes looked wild. He stood up and climbed off her. "I didn't listen last time," he said, running his fingers through his unfashionably short hair and making the tips of it stand up straight. "But I'm willing to listen to you this time. What in the blazes are you doing?"

Sarah propped herself up on her elbow, feeling a dreadful ache in her ribs. She groaned. "Ugh, you positively crushed me," she said pathetically.

"I wouldn't have had to if you hadn't run," said Carson dispassionately. He held out a hand to help Sarah up and this time, she took it gratefully, wincing as she climbed to her feet. "I'm sorry," Carson said after a moment, and he looked genuinely apologetic as he watched Sarah poke at the soreness in her ribs.

"I'm heading to the track," said Sarah as she turned away from him. "I'm going to learn to ride Averleigh in the races." She began to walk away from Carson. "And I'd appreciate it if you didn't mention any of this to my father," she added over her shoulder.

"What? You're training to be a jockey?" asked Carson. "That impossible. You'd never be allowed to enter."

"I would urge you not to worry your pretty head about me, Carson Williamson. I am a grown woman who can work out the answers to my own problems, thank you very much." Sarah still refused to look at him. She was afraid of the judgement she would see in his gray eyes. The possibility that he might return to his original idea that she was, indeed, a madwoman.

"So, that's why you're dressed like this," said Carson's voice. He was walking alongside her now, staring into her face.

"Well, I couldn't very well ride in lacy white dress now, could I?" said Sarah. She had reached the track entrance now. It was bordered by high, white fences posts on either side.

"No," said Carson, following her through the gate. "I don't suppose you could."

"Has anyone ever told you that you are very bothersome?" asked Sarah, unable to rein in her sour temper. She turned to glare at Carson, who despite the clear insult, grinned.

"I can't say that they have," he said.

"Well, you are very bothersome," she reiterated. "Do you intend to stay to witness my training session with Gibson?"

"Is that an invitation?"

"No," said Sarah firmly.

"All the same," said Carson, who was now displaying his amusement with an almost indecent zeal. "I think I will stay to watch."

With that, Carson turned and mounted the stairs that led up into the stands. Sarah watched him, incredulous, as he sank onto the nearest bench and reclined in his seat, folding his arms behind his head as though he had not a care in the world.

Sarah growled low in her throat and then stalked away from him. She approached Gibson, who was waiting for her beside the starting line. He looked worried.

"Miss Sarah?" he said, staring at Carson's smiling face just behind her.

"Shall we get started then, Gibson?" she asked nonchalantly. "I only have a few hours to spare before I'm afraid that I will be missed."

"Right away, miss," he said.

Sarah nodded sharply, and began pulling on her gloves.

"You've already got a good amount of experience riding," said Gibson, as he gave Sarah a leg up into the saddle. "I don't think it will take much for you to get used to riding Averleigh on the track. I've got her all warmed up now, so what I'm going to say is: go for it. Take her for a run and push her as fast as you can. I want to see how you do, and I'll correct you as we go."

"Really?" said Sarah nervously. She had expected a bit more information than that. "Just take her for a run?"

"Take her for a run," said Gibson grinning.

Sarah took hold of Averleigh's reins and gave her a good pat. "You hear that?" she asked. "Gibson wants us to run!"

And, ignoring the fact that Carson's eyes were fixed on her, she kicked her horse forward. Averleigh shot off over the track, and for once, Sarah wasn't the one watching from the stands. She wasn't alone, wishing it was her, her heart nearly bursting with jealousy. No, for once, she was flying!

She let out a cry of joy and kicked Averleigh faster, feeling her horse's smooth body pounding over the earth. This was completely different from riding along the coastline. This? This was easy. There was nothing in front of them but solid, even footing. She slapped the reins and Averleigh moved even faster. In a matter of second they rounded the final bend and Sarah pulled Averleigh to a slow canter beside Gibson, grinning from ear to ear.

"Look how familiar she is with you," said Gibson proudly. "She knows you so well. She'll listen to you. Now all you need to do is listen to her. Pay attention," he said. "Listen to the way she breathes. Give her a little more room with her head and she'll be able to pick up more speed."

Sarah nodded and moved her hand back on the reins.

"Good," said Gibson. "Let's give her another round."

They set off. Sarah had never felt so in tune with her horse. Averleigh's hooves pummeled the dirt, and Sarah felt as though she were shoving some deep inner despair away from her soul. Averleigh was hammering it into the ground, this sadness that she'd never even known she had.

Chapter Nine

CARSON

This was absurd. He couldn't be sitting here. He *shouldn't* be sitting here. What was he doing?

Carson sighed and rubbed the back of his neck as Sarah-Jane went soaring past him for a fourth time. Her cap had fallen off, and her long hair was streaming behind her. She looked overjoyed, transported, and very, very beautiful.

He'd been battling with himself ever since Sarah and her sister had confronted him last Saturday after the race. He'd been so stupid. So very blind. He'd been so determined that Sarah-Jane was unstable, he'd never paused to listen to her. She was right to be furious with him.

And he'd never considered that perhaps, the reason for his interest in her safety had not been merely because he thought she was a danger to herself. He was even questioning now whether he had really believed that... He'd seen how feisty she was. How much she relished in her very existence, and yet... still he had remained convinced that she *needed* him. That *he had* to do something to help her. What was wrong with him? Perhaps it was he that had gone mad.

Now though, with the question of her sanity safely out of the way, Carson was allowing himself to look at Sarah as any man in his right mind would. Especially when she kept rocketing by him with her delicious bottom encased in gentleman's trousers.

Why? Why couldn't she have worn a giant, billowing dress like any normal woman? He was becoming utterly intoxicated with the very sight of her.

"Enjoying the show?" the voice came from right beside Carson, making him jump. He recovered quickly when he realized it was Sarah's jockey. The tiny man was almost a foot shorter than himself, and half as broad.

"It is an impressive display," said Carson casually, he waved his hand nonchalantly as Sarah flew by the stands once more, trying and failing to keep them from Sarah's fine form.

"Aye, she's very good," said the man. "Much more talent than I expected her to have." He fell silent for a moment, then he said: "What are you doing here, Mr. Williamson."

Carson was surprised that the jockey knew his name. "Is that a great concern of yours, Mister...?"

"Gibson, sir."

"Gibson," repeated Carson. He was trying to appear aloof, but in reality, the man's question had struck a chord with him. What *was* he doing here? This wasn't his business. He wasn't even particularly interested in horse racing, and Miss Sarah-Jane Brittler was nothing more than an acquaintance to him.

For some reason, this thought irked him as nothing else had. What did he really know about her? This wild beauty had insnared his attention, his every waking moment, and even—he felt quite embarrassed to admit it to himself—much of his sleep as well.

"Actually," Carson hadn't realized that the man, Gibson, was still speaking. "It is very concerning to me sir, not least because I am staking my reputation on this little lady," he nodded his head to the place were Sarah and her horse galloped in the distance. "But I am not so concerned about myself... not as much as I am about her. You see..." he paused, seeming to gather his thoughts. "She's a smart girl, sir. She knows how much she stands to loose if anyone were to... er... inform on her, sir."

Carson looked up. "You think I intend to speak to her father?"

Gibson had pulled off his cap. He was twisting it in his hands, looking unnerved. "Sir, what you have to understand is... she... she could win this thing. Just look at her," he pointed to Sarah as she pulled Averleigh to a halt and urged her to the nearby trough. She was ginning from ear to ear. "I timed her quarter. Averleigh made a nineteen second round with Sarah on her back. She's never done anything like that before. Not with me, not with anyone. If you tell a soul... she'll be ruined."

Carson stared at Gibson. His mind oddly blank. "What do you mean, ruined?"

"Sir," said Gibson, sitting down beside Carson and fixing him with a determined stare. "Women aren't allowed to ride in the races. Forget allowed. She'd be a laughing stock. Her family would be splashed all over the newspaper headlines. No one can ever find out about this, she'd never forgive herself."

Carson glanced over at Sarah-Jane, who was still beaming, her small, gentle fingers now combing through Averleigh's carefully braided mane. "I hadn't realized the seriousness of the situation," he said, drawing away from Gibson and sitting up straight. He imagined the way Sarah would look at him if she found out he gave her away. He imagined the happy smile falling from her pretty face; saw her bright blue eyes filling up with tears. She would never forgive him if he stole this from her.

"I won't breathe a word," he said to Gibson. "Not to anyone."

Sarah looked up at him as he said this. It was as though his words had carried across the vast space between them, as though his promise had echoed into her heart, although there was no way she could possibly have heard him. He wondered what she was thinking. Was she scared for herself? Scared of him? She must have realized the danger of allowing him to follow her today. He gave a small half-wave in her direction. Sarah turned away from him.

He smiled grimly.

Gibson was still eyeing him. After a moment, he grinned wickedly. "You...er... a little bit sweet on Miss Sarah?" he asked, a hint of suggestion in his tone.

"No," said Carson stoutly.

Gibson's grin widened. He clapped Carson on the shoulder. "She's a fiery one, Mr. Williamson. I hope you know what you've got yourself into." And on that enigmatic note, he climbed to his small feet and strode away, skipping on every other step.

Carson watched him go, his chest somehow lighter than it had been before.

By the end of Sarah and Gibson's little training session, something had solidified in Carson's mind. A fact. He was interested in courting Sarah-Jane Brittler. More than interested. He felt a pull towards her that was unlike anything he had ever known, and now that he had accepted this, a series of actions would be required for him to win her over. Which he would do, of course. Once Carson had decided to make Sarah-Jane his, the whole thing seemed remarkably simpler.

First, he had to apologize. Really, truly, deeply apologize to her for their disastrous first encounter and his behavior thereafter. And if he wasn't much mistaken, judging by the way Sarah continued to wince and hold at her ribs, he owed her another serious apology for knocking her to the ground earlier today. He flinched slightly as he watched her massaging her stomach through the man's shirt she wore. What had come over him?

All Carson knew was that Sarah had been escaping him. Pulling away. Flying away from him, and he couldn't stand to let that happen. Not again. And... so...he had leapt. Rather harder than he had meant to, actually. He remembered the feel of her underneath him as she wriggled and shrieked, attempting to evade him, and a dull flush crept up the back of his neck.

Drat those clothes on her fine form, they weren't fooling anyone. He averted his eyes as Sarah sauntered towards him, trying not to picture how delightful her slender hips had felt between his large hands.

"We're calling it a day," she said saucily, crossing her arms over her chest and staring down at him with something akin to loathing in her eyes. "I have to return home before I am missed."

Carson stood up. "You'll have to wear something different next time," he said without thinking.

"Excuse me?" she said sourly, and her eyes flashed.

"Sarah," he said, and for a moment, a bit of the exhaustion he was carrying around with him leaked into his voice. "Those clothes are hiding nothing." His eyes skated over her body of their own accord, and he saw her arms tighten uncomfortably over her chest. He grinned, enjoying the way she squirmed. "Any man within a mile would be able to tell that you're a woman."

He tried not to put too much emphasis on the word. She was looking very womanly. Very...tempting. With her hair undone and her cheeks flushing a pretty pink as he made her more aware of herself.

"Very well," she said. Her voice was icy. "I shall come better prepared next time. Good day to you, Mr. Williamson."

"Wait," he said, and he reached for her arm to stop her from leaving. She glared pointedly, and he released her. "I'm sorry. It's just..." he wanted a reason for her to stay. He wanted to talk to her. To make things right. "Would you mind if I accompanied you?"

"Yes," she muttered, and she began to stroll away from him. He watched her hips for a moment and then caught up to her.

"Yes, you mind? Or yes, I may accompany you?"

"Yes, I mind," she said casting him a sideways look and quickening her pace.

"Why?" he asked. They descended the small set of stairs that led onto the track. Gibson was a few feet away, readying Averleigh for the ride back to the Brittler's private livery.

"Why?" she repeated, sounding incredulous. "You must be joking, Mr. Williamson."

"But I'm not," he said. He couldn't help but grin at her. She was adorably flustered now. He skipped a few steps ahead of her and then turned right around, walking backward so that he could see her face.

"Let's just stop to think," she said. She was glaring at him. "In the very short time that we have been acquainted, I have developed more serious bruises than my cousin Harrison in England. Do you know what he does? He's a circus performer!"

"What?" laughed Carson, completed sidetracked. "You've a cousin that is a circus performer?"

"Don't change the subject," snapped Sarah, coloring up.

"I didn't. You did."

Sarah acted as though she had not heard him. She held up five fingers in front of his face. "You've insulted me," she said bluntly, putting down a finger. "You've knocked me off a cliff." She put down another finger.

"Well... that's a bit of an over statement," said Carson, sobering up at once. Again, Sarah ignored him. She was still moving forward. Carson glanced behind himself to make sure he wasn't about to run into anything.

"You absolutely refused to listen to anything I said until my elder sister came to my aid. You've practically *black-mailed* me into a courtship," she said. "Aaannd," she continued furiously, talking over him as he made to interrupt.

"You've seriously endangered my family's reputation with your incessant nosiness," she finished, putting down the final finger so that her fist was balled under his nose. "Now tell me, Mr. Williamson," she stopped, her breast heaving with the ferocity of her outburst "Why, when I've a pleasant, unencumbered walk ahead of me, free from any injury or insult, would I choose to subjugate myself to your presence?"

Carson grinned and shrugged wryly, "In all honesty, Miss Brittler, you would have to be quite mad to accept my company."

Sarah stared at him for a full ten seconds, and for a moment, Carson thought that she might explode. But then she threw back her head and laughed. It was a beautiful sound. It was the sound of encouragement to Carson's ears. Encouragement and relief.

"Fine then," said Sarah-Jane once she had giggled herself into silence. She took hold of his arm and steered him toward the track exit. "Then I suppose I must be mad after all, lead on Mr. Williamson."

They walked beside Gibson, whose smirk was much too broad for Carson's taste, to the edge of the track.

"Thank you, Gibson," said Sarah, "this was fantastic. Is there anything I need to bear in mind until next time?"

"Just watch your grip, Miss. Averleigh's used to having you on her back. It won't take long before you're both ready."

"Same time next week?" she asked him.

He nodded as he closed and locked the the gate, and Carson guided Sarah up the narrow walk that led back into town.

They moved in silence for a few moments. Carson felt strangely at his ease. He began humming as they climbed a steep slope.

"I haven't forgiven you, you know," said Sarah-Jane suddenly.

"No?" responded Carson airily. "You certainly seem more accommodating than before."

"You caught me in a moment of weakness," she said. "I can assure you that all is not forgotten between us."

"Why can't it be?" Carson stopped to help Sarah-Jane negotiate her way up a particularly gravelly portion of the path.

"For each and every one of the reasons I have just told you," she said, and Carson sensed that her mood was turning sour again. "And a dozen others besides."

"Well now," said Carson, "I'll have to do something to remedy that then, won't I?"

"I highly doubt there is anything that you can do to change my opinion of you, sir," said Sarah haughtily. She adjusted the belt she wore around her men's trousers. "How do you wear these things," she grumbled, looking at his. "It keeps sliding around."

"It's too big for you," said Carson, and he reached for her waist. "Come here." Sarah stumbled into his hands as he gave her a small yank and he gripped her firmly, trying not to notice how good she felt beneath his fingers.

He unfastened her belt buckle, and pulled out his knife, using it to cut another notch in the leather. He heard her breathing hitch. "There," he said, fastening it again and releasing her. "How does that feel?"

"Will you quite tossing me around willy-nilly?" she grouched, adjusting her belt and straightening her cotton shirt. "I've had quite enough of that, thank you. Where did you learn your manners from?"

"England," said Carson matter-of-factly, starting up the slope once more. "And a bit in Paris too," he added after a moment of thought.

"Well, if my mother is any indication," said Sarah scrambling up after him, "the women in London wouldn't take very kindly to being seized and tackled and whatever else."

"You might be surprised," muttered Carson. Amusement crept into his tone, despite his best effort.

"What did you say?" said Sarah. He had his back to her.

Carson looked over his shoulder and his heart leapt into his throat. The sun was low in the late afternoon sky, hovering over the coast and its many beach goers in the distance.

He hadn't realized how close they were to the crowds.

"You better get your hat back on," he said quickly. Sarah looked around, and then shoved her cap onto her head, tucking her hair into place.

"Honestly," he said staring at her. "You'd be more in-conspicuous if you were wearing a potato sack. Get in front of me. We better get you to your carriage before anyone spots you."

Chapter Ten

SARAH

"Well, of course I have to accompany you," said her mother, stalking over to the kitchen window and peering through drapes, as though checking to see if any of the neighbors had their ears pressed to the glass. "What sort of mother would I be if I allowed my daughter to run off to a man's house unescorted?"

"We wouldn't be unescorted, Mother," grumbled Sarah, stabbing moodily at her eggs. "Dianna would be with us."

"No. Absolutely not. If you're going to visit Mr. Williamson's home, I'm coming with you. In fact, I think your father might like to join us. Yes," she nodded her head as though the matter was settled. "I'm sure he would be interested to see the progress Carson has made on the construction."

Sarah groaned as her mother left the kitchen. "It could have been worse," said Noelle consolingly, patting Sarah's shoulder. "At least she hasn't told you that Mr. Williamson will now be courting *her* instead of *you.*"

The girls broke into peals of laughter that echoed around the tiny room. The cook, Marcia, entered the kitchen, looking rather stern, and their giggles were quickly stifled in their breakfast plates.

The next day Sarah donned a brand new riding habit of sturdy, burgundy material and turned to gaze at herself in the mirror. She was beginning to see what Carson had meant the last time they had spoken.

Last night she had stood here in front of her mirror, spinning slowly on the spot as she examined her reflection. She had been wearing a large, billowy nightgown, but even so, it could not disguise the distinctly feminine curve of her hips and bosom.

She flushed, remembering the way Carson's eyes had focused on those curves. Never in her life had a man been so bold. It was outrageous. And yet... and yet... it was somehow... flattering.

"I don't see why we all have to come," came a grumble from the doorway and Noelle pushed her way into Sarah's bedroom without bothering to knock. "He's clearly already chosen his favorite from the four of us."

Charlotte entered behind their youngest sister, looking much more dignified. "I'm not sure we should be going at all," she said, sitting down on Sarah's bed and smoothing her lavender skirts. "He's a strange man, isn't he, Sarah?"

"He is a bit strange, yes," she agreed, turning away from the mirror.

"Have you been pinching your cheeks?" asked Noelle, her wide eyes darting over Sarah's face. "You're all pink."

"Are your stays too tight again?"

"No," said Sarah hurriedly. "I'm just a bit warm. I'll cool down on the ride over."

"So Di tells us that Mr. Williamson has given up the idea that you're deranged?" said Charlotte, scrutinizing her cooley from the bed.

"So it would seem," sighed Sarah. She straightened a pin in her hair.

"And what? He's decided that since you're not mad, he would quite like to court you?"

"You know," said Sarah, a hair pin sticking out of her mouth, "it was so easy for Dianna to convince him that I was not mad, that I wonder if he ever truly believed it himself."

Noelle brought a finger up to her chin. "Now, there's a thought. What a way to get to know someone."

It was difficult to contain Averleigh as they cantered alongside the carriage that held her mother and sisters. She was used to the breakneck journeys around the track, and it wasn't quite as much fun to trot complacently along the streets towards Carson's manorhouse.

It was an overcast, murky sort of day, not at all ideal for a ride around Mr. Williamson's large estate, but when he had asked, Sarah had been hard put to say no. It was infuriating. One moment he was her worst enemy. Someone she would rather kick than say "how do you do?" to in the marketplace. Now he was a charmer, interested in everything she was doing, and Sarah was charmed.

He's playing you like a puppet, she thought to herself. But she couldn't seem to help it. In spite of everything. In spite of every reason she had just given him the day before, she found herself looking forward to being in his company.

He was a smug, pompous, arrogant fool to be sure. But... he was hers, in a way.

Sarah had very little experience with secrets, but she was beginning to fall under the impression that they brought people closer together. What else could exert such a powerful influence on her feelings? It must be the secrets lying between her and Carson that were pulling them together.

Sarah-Jane couldn't wrap her head around this thought, so she tried her very best to stop thinking about Carson Williamson.

This proved to be rather difficult.

"Watch your step," said Carson on greeting them in doorway of his home. "You've come at a good time. The workers have just gone on break, you'll be able to see what they're working on."

They had arrived at the address he had provided Sarah the day before to see a simple, but elegant, brick front house. It stood two stories tall, and the front yard was bordered on all sides by wide hedges that came nearly to the top of the eaves.

Neatly trimmed flowering crabapple trees decorated each side of the garden path that led up to the front door. Their blossoms danced over the lawn in a slight breeze. Overall, the effect was pleasing, although the place had a vague air of neglect about it.

Samantha Brittler gasped as she stepped over the threshold. "It's magnificent," she said.

"It's definitely better than it was when I arrived," said Carson sheepishly. He stood to the side, ushering the rest of the family into the foyer.

"You purchased it directly from the bank?" asked Thomas Brittler, stepping gingerly around a thick canvas sheet to peer into the room adjacent.

"Well, I had an inspection done while I was still overseas. The bones of the house are sound. It's mostly cosmetic."

Sarah stood in the back of the group, looking around interestedly. Somehow, she found it very hard to picture Carson here, in this vast house all alone. The walls were all painted a faded white, and the carpet underfoot was musty and smelled of mildew.

Accentuated perhaps by the darkly stained wood that decorated the stair banisters and all the windows, the place seemed to seep with shadows.

Thomas Brittler was nodding. Her father was one of those unusual people who could see past the surface of things. Houses, people, horses, land. He was always able to look at something diminished and see infinite opportunity for the betterment of it.

"Yes," he was saying. "Yes, I can see what you mean." He lifted his fist and knocked on the nearest wall. "Might we have a little poke around?"

"Please," said Carson, gesturing to the next room. He stood back and held the canvas aside as Sarah's mother, father and sisters passed, but when Sarah came close to him, he brushed his fingers over the back of her dress and followed her.

"You look quite lovely today," he whispered in her ear, low enough that the rest of her family would not catch it. "Although, I must say," he added suggestively, as his eyes traveled over the back of her skirts, "I do miss the trousers."

Sarah flushed, and deliberately rammed her elbow into his chest.

Carson grunted, causing Noelle to turn around and examine him with some concern, but he managed to turn it into a hacking cough.

Sarah took the opportunity to examined her surroundings. The room they had stepped into was plainly in a state of near completion. A fireplace mantle had been set into the far wall, and although the floors were still bare, the walls had been paneled in rich oak.

"I'm sick of the dust," he said a little louder. "The hammering. The saws. It's enough to drive anyone up the wall."

"I'd imagine so," crooned Samantha sympathetically. "Don't you have anywhere you could stay until the renovations are finished? The Hotel at Brighton Beach is very fashionable this time of year."

"That was the original plan," Carson responded. He rubbed discreetly at the place on his chest where Sarah's elbow had connected. "But I foolishly decided that I would like to be on hand during the construction."

"Well that's just absolutely ridiculous," said Samantha. "Have you called the Hotel? I'm sure they would have a room for you."

"Yes, actually." Carson took several steps into the room, looking around it with dry amusement. "I contacted them yesterday evening to see whether they had any availability, but they weren't able to accommodate me."

"What a pity," said Thomas. He was still looking around with interest.

Samantha started to say something, but Thomas had drawn back the curtains covering the one of the windows. Sarah watched the shadows flee into the corners as the curtain hissed over the brass rod, illuminating the intricately spiraling dust clouds that filled the room.

"So, this room will be your study?" asked Thomas.

"Yes, I think so," responded Carson. His heavy footsteps echoed dismally in the empty space as he strode over to Thomas. "It's nearly done. The flooring comes next, I think, and they already have a few men working in the hall. I'm hoping we shall see completion by the end of the summer, or close to it."

"Good, very good," said Thomas approvingly.

Carson took the family through each of the rooms in his house. "The construction on the master bedroom, naturally, was finished before I even left London," he said, lighting an oil lamp on the stand next to the bed.

Sarah felt her eyebrows fly up, despite herself. She'd never been in a man's bedroom before. The room was sparsely furnished. The bed was large, but simply made of dark mahogany. Two windows sat on either side of another fireplace. The grate was full of ash and embers, which glowed eerily out of the semi-darkness of the room like the eyes of a cat.

Overall, the house was very beautiful, set to be impressive once the renovations were completed, but it lacked a certain charm. A certain something that would give it a warm, friendly feeling of welcome. Sarah pondered at this as Carson led the family out onto the back terrace.

"The property stretches from here to the coastline in the back," he said without much enthusiasm. "There is a set of ruins that stands on the along the cliffs there. It belonged to my great, great, grandfather, several hundred years ago."

At the mention of the ruins, Sarah went as red as the bricks on the house just behind her, and stared determinedly towards the neighbor's yard, which they could just make out through the line of hedges a good distance away.

She could feel Carson's eyes on her, and knew he was grinning. Her sisters too had become oddly giggly. She glared at Noelle, who quieted at once. Dianna and Charlotte were both smirking at her, but she ignored them.

"I'm afraid that is where the tour ends," Carson said. He spread his arms wide. "Here is my humbled abode. I hope that it will be more to look at the next time you join me for lunch."

"It really is quite impressive already," said the girls' mother, staring at Carson with something close to admiration in her eyes. "The way you've taken something so derelict and turned it into a fabulous home. It reminds me of Thomas," she said fondly, giving her husband's arm a soft pinch.

Thomas's shoulders jumped slightly as he let out a chuckle. "Yes, I like the way you can see past the mundane, Carson. That's the individual spirit a true entrepreneur needs in this world."

Carson accepted the praise with a nod. "I thank you for your complements Mister and Missus Brittler," he said. "Shall we get settled in? I'll have the staff bring up a tray."

With a murmur of agreement, the Brittler's all took seats around the large outdoor dining table and fell into quiet chatter as Carson went in search of lunch.

"Well," muttered Dianna in Sarah's ear, "I'm impressed."

"With what?" demanded Sarah, a little testily.

Dianna was still smirking. "Your beau has made quite a home for himself," she said suggestively.

"He's not my beau," said Sarah.

"You had better inform him of that fact, my dear sister," responded Dianna with a tinkling laugh that echoed across the back lawn. "Because I don't think he knows it."

"What makes you say that?" snapped Sarah, crossing her arms in front of her chest, as though hoping to protect herself from any further accusations.

Dianna snorted derisively. "Come on Sarah, even you must have noticed that he could hardly take his eyes off you."

Sarah blushed crimson again.

She was still pink when Carson returned to the group.

"They have everything ready," he said, glancing a Sarah, who continued to avoid his gaze. "Lunch will be up in just a moment."

"Wonderful," said Samantha, clapping her hands together. "Now, listen. Thomas and I have just been talking, and we've agreed that you should come and stay with us this Summer."

If there had been any air left in the day, Sarah-Jane would have sucked it into her lungs in shock. However, the back terrace seemed to have become temporarily airless.

"Oh, no, Mrs. Brittler. No. I thank you. I wouldn't want to impose," said Carson. He glanced at Sarah. As she met his eyes, she felt her own widen. He was grinning. Evilly. Mischievously. As though he knew exactly what Sarah was thinking.

Sarah raised her brows discreetly, and gave her head the smallest of shakes. *Don't you dare*, she thought. *Don't you do it.*

"But it wouldn't be an imposition at all," cried Samantha. She beamed around at her daughters. "We'd be delighted to have you, wouldn't we girls? There's still two empty rooms in our summer cottage. They aren't being used at all. You could have your pick of them."

Carson sighed, looking put upon. "I really couldn't Mrs. Brittler. It's very kind of you to offer..." but his eyes were laughing.

Sarah swelled with fury, breathing heavily out of her nostrils.

"I insist!" said Samantha, firmly. "You can bring your things over this evening."

"You're sure it won't be an imposition," said Carson most convincingly.

"My dear boy, I would be offended if you did not join us," said Samantha.

"Yes, quite," agreed Thomas.

Sarah couldn't believe her parents. They were both looking at Carson Williamson as though he were a precocious two-year old.

The food arrived, and Carson was staring smugly across the table at Sarah, and she could do nothing but sit there in silence and seethe.

"You did that on purpose," hissed Sarah. It was late afternoon and she and Carson were climbing into their saddles.

"Did what?" he asked innocently, giving her a leg up onto Averleigh's back and letting his hands linger far too long.

"You... I don't know how you did it, but I know you did it on purpose." Sarah adjusted her skirts in a flurry and settled herself more securely into the saddle.

"I don't know what you're talking about," said Carson, and he grinned as he egged his horse around the path that led to the back of his house. "Are you sure you won't come with us?" he called to Sarah's family, who were all lounging comfortable around the back terrace.

"Oh no, that's quite alright," said Thomas, waving over his head with a deck of cards in his hand. Her father was never one to abandon a card game. "You go on ahead. You say the property just stretches to the coastline?"

"Yes, sir," said Carson. He was looking elated, and very handsome. His hair had grown out a bit. It was no longer cropped short to his head, it was an inch or two longer and a dark, rich brown. Absurdly, Sarah found herself wanting to sink her fingers into it, to discover if it truly was as soft as it looked. "Very well," Carson was saying. "Leland, why don't you accompany us? Miss Sarah and I can hardly go on our own."

Sarah saw her mother's eyebrows fly up at this, and she could tell she had expected Carson to take advantage of the rest of the family wanting to stay behind.

"Right you are, sir," called the butler who had brought out the lunch. "I'll be just a moment."

Fifteen minutes later, Sarah—a frown firmly plastered on her face—was following after Carson's dappled gray mare as she disappeared down a narrow path through the trees. Averleigh was tugging at the reigns in Sarah's hands, eager to pick up the pace.

"Easy," she whispered to her. "We need to go easy to-day."

Behind them, the butler, Leland, could be heard as he huffed and puffed his way through the underbrush on the back of a chestnut. He seemed inexperienced on a horse and Sarah was reminded of the time she had tried to get Dianna to ride alongside her at a festival. The memory brought a brief smile to her lips.

When the path widened, Sarah brought Averleigh up alongside Carson and fixed him with a beady eye.

"What sort of game are you playing, Carson?"

"Miss Sarah-Jane," he said, and he pulled his horse to a halt so abruptly that Averleigh trotted past him.

Sarah turned her horse around so that she could still see Carson, who was grinning again, and looking devilishly handsome in the half-light of the trees.

"It is my full intention to make you fall in love with me," he stated.

Sarah stared at him. This wasn't the first time that his straightforwardness had taken her by surprise, and she had a the distinct impression that it wouldn't be the last.

"Oh." She couldn't think of anything else to say for a moment. Carson was watching her. His smile was so compellingly mischievous. It was as though he were attempting to convince her to partake in some grand adventure with him. "I'm not sure that is at all advisable," she almost whispered.

"It is the truth," he said, shrugging. "You wanted to know my *game*," he said. "There is no game. I have developed an interest in you. That," he added, nudging his horse a little closer to her. "Is a fact."

Sarah narrowed her eyes at him. "An interest?" she said blithely. "Is that so?"

"Yes," said Carson, as though she were being difficult. "It is."

"You think your *interest* is enough to win my heart, Carson Williamson?"

Carson paused, cocking his head to the side, examining her. "I don't know," he said quietly.

Sarah shook her head. "You have a very long way to go," she said. And with that she spun her horse around and trotted away up the path.

They hadn't been riding for long when the area began to look familiar to her and Sarah sighed. There it was at last. It had been far too long. The ruins stood, still crumbling and weathered, overlooking the sea with a obstinate determination that would not be shaken. The stones of the foundation seemed to be saying: "We've stood here for three hundred years. We'll stand here three hundred more."

Sarah didn't pause to wait for Carson or his man. She nudged Averleigh through the wide archway on the ground floor and dismounted. Averleigh snuffled, apparently delighted to find herself in this familiar place, and she lowered her head to graze.

Nothing had changed since she'd last saw it. Every pebble seemed to have frozen in time while she was away. She brushed her hands over the rough stones that scratched lightly at her fingertips, wandering towards her favorite place.

Sarah could feel the exact moment when Carson entered the ruins. The air seemed to shift. Her private sanctuary was being invaded once more. She tried not to notice as Carson dismounted and began to follow her. His pace crunching over the stone-strewn floor.

Sarah changed her course abruptly. As she circled a dilapidated chimneypiece, she darted behind the wall. She heard Carson approach and then stop. "Sarah?" he called, and his voice was lost beneath the sound of the ocean waves.

She giggled, and slid away from him.

"Sarah?" he called again, and she saw him come around the corner. Laughing, she dodged around a stone pillar and hid, pressing her fingers to her lips to stifle her giggles.

She didn't hear him approaching. Curious to see where he had gone, she peered around her pillar, her eyes searching.

"What are you doing?" Carson's voice made her jump. He had come around the other side, and was now gazing at her with undisguised curiosity.

"What's the matter, Carson?" Sarah asked coyly. "Don't you know how to have any fun at all?"

"Perhaps your idea of fun is different from mine," he said, folding his arms over his chest.

"Tell me then," said Sarah, planting her hands behind her and leaning against the pillar. "What is your idea of fun?"

Carson was watching her. Birds twittered overhead as the silence stretched between them. He looked calm, almost detached.

"I must say," he whispered after a moment. "There wasn't much cause for fun back in London."

"Truly?" Sarah raised her eyebrows. "It sounds like such a dreadful place. I don't think I will ever choose to visit."

"No? I have family back in London."

Sarah's eyes were taking in the dark blue of Carson's. He looked windswept, and again, she was put in mind of a young sea captain, readying himself to set out on his first voyage. He was so very handsome. His chin was dotted with fresh stubble, and his eyes were dancing merrily.

He was very close to her now and he was inching closer still. There was less than an arm's length between them now. "London itself can be quite unpleasant," he conceded. "But the company and the countryside are both enjoyable."

"Even so," whispered Sarah. "I don't think I would ever like to visit."

"You may change you mind one day."

"I don't think so," said Sarah, and she spun away from him.

She meandered up the crumbling staircase, looking back over her shoulder to see if Carson would follow her. He did.

"Do you have views like this in London, Mr. Williamson?" she asked as he came to stand beside her, gazing out at the gray ocean waves.

"No," he said, leaning against the stone frame. He was looking at her. "I can't say that we do." She caught his eye, and he did not turn away. "I'm sorry," he said at last. "I don't think you will ever understand how very sorry I am for the many mistakes that I have made regarding you."

"Thank you for saying that," she whispered.

He took a step nearer to her. "I never should have assumed someone like you would be anything other than what she said she was."

Sarah said nothing. She wasn't really sure how to respond.

"You've entrusted me with something special this last week," he continued.

"You didn't exactly leave me a choice," laughed Sarah.

"Nevertheless," he said. "I will not betray the trust you have placed in me." Carson took another step towards her. "Is there some chance, in the future, that you might find it in your heart to forgive me?"

Sarah frowned, pretending to contemplate. "Perhaps," she said, then she smiled wickedly up at him. "In the very distant future."

"Then I will not loose hope," chuckled Carson, and he kissed her.

Sarah was on fire. She lost her grip on the stone behind her as Carson's arms encircled her in an embrace so warm that it was like kissing the sun. She could feel every inch of her body heating to his touch. And he held her so lightly, so gently. His hands slid around her waist and tugged her tightly against his chest, and he brought a hand up under her chin to tilt back her head, deepening the kiss.

"I'm sorry," said Carson suddenly. He stepped away so abruptly that Sarah nearly toppled. He seized her and steadied her. "Please don't fall again," he said, sounding annoyed.

Sarah laughed. "If you insist on startling me every time I visit this place, I'm afraid I will have to forbid you from joining me, else it will my death."

He stepped away from her, still looking apologetic. "I forgot myself," he said.

"Mr. Williamson," purred Sarah, in a deep throaty voice that she had never heard herself use before. "If you forgot yourself more often, perhaps you would learn how to have a bit of fun."

A cough echoed from below and Sarah flushed. She had all but forgotten that they were not alone. Carson glared toward the massive hole in the second story. "I told him to wait outside," he muttered distractedly.

"Maybe he thought you meant something different."

"Yes, and maybe he's a right nosey blockhead," he said irritatedly. "Come on, we had better get back before we're missed."

Chapter Eleven

Carson

Really, he ought to be congratulated. Carson hummed cheerfully as he packed his suitcase. Sarah-Jane Brittler was a fascinating woman. Very beautiful and unique in every respect, and he had just secured an invitation to stay with her family for the remainder of the summer.

He was excited. The first phase of his plan had just taken place. He had successfully apologized to Sarah for their disastrous first encounter and his subsequent behavior, and he didn't think that his apology had been badly received either.

He recalled, with startlingly vivid detail, how Sarah had felt in his arms. How she had fit there...perfectly, as though she had been molded for him.

Carson paused in the act of pulling on his overcoat and glanced around his sparse bedroom. He wouldn't be sorry to leave it behind, at least until the construction was finished. His new home lacked warmth. It was equipped with the essentials, nothing more, and its blank walls stared accusingly at him while he snapped his suitcase closed and headed out the door.

"Mr. Williamson," said the Brittler's butler, bowing him into the house. "The Mister and Missus are awaiting you in the drawing room. Shall I take up your luggage?"

"Yes, please, I thank you," said Carson, and he proceeded down the narrow hall to greet his hosts.

"Mr. Williamson, how lovely, we were just settling down for a nightcap. Can I tempt you?"

"Please," said Carson, and he allowed Thomas Brittler to pour him a large glass of brandy.

The three of them sat down in the comfortable seats closest to the fire. "Now," said Thomas, fixing Carson with a penetrating stare. "Let us speak plainly, Mr. Williamson."

Carson turned in his chair to face Thomas, aware that Samantha Brittler was watching him closely.

"Of course, sir. As you might have noticed, deception is not my strong suit."

"Well," chuckled Thomas appreciatively, "quite right." He took a sip of the amber colored liquid in his glass, and the firelight glinted off the gold band he wore on his left ring finger. Carson found his eyes following the ring as Thomas allowed his hand to rest on the arm of his chair. "You told us at the offset that you were in need of a wife."

"I still am, sir," responded Carson with a small smile, and Sarah-Jane's beautiful face flashed in front of his eyes.

"Yes, I thought you might be," said Thomas. "Am I wrong in thinking that you have set your sights on our Sarah-Jane?"

Carson's smile broadened. He liked Thomas Brittler very much. The man reminded him of his own father. Straight-forward, no nonsense. "No, sir, you would be correct."

"Yes," said Thomas, "I thought so. The thing is, Mr. Williamson, I wish you be quite plain with you indeed."

"Alright," said Carson slowly, wondering what this could possibly be about.

"I love all of my daughters equally," Thomas began, and as he spoke, he settled back into his seat. "I would you like you to be aware of the fact that my girls are not bargaining chips to me. I will not treat them as such."

"I wouldn't expect you to," said Carson, now feeling truly at a loss. His grip around his glass was relaxed, but his foot was tapping nervously.

Thomas nodded gravely. "It will not matter what you offer me for her hand," he said. "I don't care what sort of plan you have waiting in the wings. I will not allow you to marry Sarah-Jane if she does not love you."

Carson felt his body relax. "Sir, I would never ask you to do such a thing. Although I have very little experience in the matter, and my father never remarried after my mother died," he saw Samantha Brittler shift uncomfortably in her seat. "I am a firm believer that a marriage cannot be treated as merely a business transaction. There has to be feeling and emotion involved, otherwise how could the couple ever be expected to flourish?"

"Quite," said Thomas Brittler, looking very pleased that Carson had caught on so quickly. He folded his hands around his brandy glass and surveyed Carson fondly, as though he was perfectly comfortable sitting here with him and discussing matters of the heart.

This was something his father had never done. Not ever. And strangely, Carson felt a sudden kinship with the man before him. Thomas Brittler was still an unknown entity, still unusual in his ways, but Carson couldn't help but feel a small bit of relief at knowing that he was not alone in allowing his heart to play a part in his future. Thomas obviously had, and look at what he had now.

Four beautiful daughters, and wife who, for all her showiness and austerity, seemed to love him and respect him just as much as he did her.

Yes, Thomas Brittler had obviously done something right.

Breakfast the next day was laughably enjoyable. Carson had a difficult time retaining a straight face. He joined the family in the morning, and spent a good portion of the meal stroking Sarah-Jane's hand beneath the table and watching her cheeks turn pink.

"Are you going to do that every day?" she asked him irritably later that afternoon as they took a slow turn around the garden.

"That depends?" said Carson, examining a rose bush with interest.

"On what?"

"Oh, a great number of things," he said, turning to face her seriously. "Most of them revolving around you happening to look quite as delicious as my breakfast. It's very distracting, you know," he added, his tone light and airy. "If you don't want to be touched, you will have to try to look less appealing." He gathered her small hand into his as he said this and pressed a kiss onto the back of her knuckles. "Although, I've seen you sporting men's clothing, so I think the possibility of you being unappealing is sorely limited."

Sarah tugged her fingers from his grasp, but she did not look as grumpy as he thought she might. "You're a flatterer, Mr. Williamson, and I cannot seem to decide if your outlandishly forward statements are designed to charm me or to irritate me."

Carson shrugged, trying to hide his smile. "Perhaps a bit of both?"

Sarah whacked him playfully with her fan. "I cannot imagine why you would want to do both."

"Oh ho, Miss Sarah, and you thought I didn't know how to have fun," laughed Carson, and then he dodged out of the way as the fan came swooshing towards his face once more.

"Mister Williamson? Miss Sarah?"

The harsh whisper came from somewhere near the garden gate and both he and Sarah looked around.

"Gibson!" Sarah cried.

"What in the depths of...Gibson! What's happened to you, old boy?" They rushed to the man's side.

The small jockey looked distinctly the worse for wear. Both his eyes were black with heavy bruising, and his nose was steadily dripping blood, but that wasn't the worst of it. As Carson looked down, he saw that Gibson was leaning heavily to one side. His shoulder was twisted at an awkward angle that made Carson's stomach squirm.

"Quick, quick," Sarah was saying. "Get the carriage. We have to get him to the doctor straight away."

Five minutes later, they were lifting a limp Gibson into the back of the Brittler's carriage. He had fainted.

"Did he say anything else?" Carson asked Sarah.

"No, he went down as soon as you'd gone. I barely caught him," she laid an anxious hand on her friend's forehead as Carson clambered up beside them both and banged on the carriage roof. It set off.

"What do you think happened to him?"

"I don't have a clue. Do you think his horse threw him?"

"But why would he come here?" asked Sarah in a panic.

"Maybe he was at the livery. It's just around the corner from here."

Sarah nodded, but he didn't think she had really heard him. She was gazing at Gibson's injuries.

"Look at this," she said suddenly. "Look, just here. What is that?"

"It looks like the imprint of a ring," said Carson. He ran his finger over the indent in Gibson's left cheek. The carriage gave an unfortunate jolt, and Carson gripped the leather of the seat to keep himself from falling over onto the jockey.

"Someone hit him? Who?"

"Who knows," said Carson with a shrug. "Maybe he got into a disagreement in a bar?"

"I don't know," said Sarah worriedly.

The journey to the doctor's hospital seemed to take ages, and when they arrived, Carson leapt out of the carriage before it had even stopped moving. Gibson groaned as the orderlies lifted him onto a stretcher and brought him inside.

"What happened to him?" asked the doctor, lifting Gibson's eyelids and prodding his injuries.

"No idea," whispered Sarah, she seemed close to tears.

Wordlessly, Carson held out his hand to her and she grasped it gratefully, breathing hard.

They waited for over an hour in the hospital, speaking only to worry aloud what was happening. At last, the doctor came into the room.

"Your friend has had a nasty fall of some sort. If I didn't know any better, I'd think he'd been attacked."

"He very well might have been," said Sarah vehemently, and the doctor looked at her with raised eyebrows.

"We'll keep him here for as long as we can. He's breathing well, and we were able to maneuver his shoulder back into place. He'll be in quite a bit of pain for a good long time, but hopefully it will heal alright. As for his head injury, I can't say on that."

"What do you mean 'you can't say'?" asked Sarah-Jane, sounding startled. "He'll be alright, won't he?"

The doctor shook his head. "It's in God's hands, miss."

Sarah gasped and sat down very fast.

"Thank you," said Carson numbly to the doctor. The man turned away, but Carson's mind was already whirring.

"I'll be back," he said.

"Where are you going?" asked Sarah, alarmed.

"First, I'm going to send a message to your family and tell them where we've gone. Secondly, I'm going to head over to the racecourse and talk to a few of Gibson's friends. Maybe one of them will know what has happened to him."

Carson was as good as his word. He had a sneaking suspicion that he knew what had happened to Gibson, and he was determined to find out who was responsible.

There were only two jockeys on the course when he arrived and both of them were moving so fast that neither of them spotted Carson until they'd rode by him three consecutive times.

"Whoa," one of them shouted, and he slowed, looking down at Carson. "The race isn't until next weekend, pal," he said shortly. "You shouldn't be here."

"I'm not much for racing," said Carson fixing the man with a look of frank curiosity. "Do either of you know a man that goes by the name of Gibson?"

"What's going on?" the second jockey had slowed and now trotted his horse up to meet Carson.

"I was just asking your friend if either of you knew a man called Gibson."

The second jockey, a wiry man with quite a lot of neck, looked uneasily at his companion. "We know him," he said slowly. "He alright?"

"Why wouldn't he be alright?" Carson asked, raising a hand to shield his eyes from the glare of the setting sun.

The jockeys exchanged another look. Carson frowned up at them. "Mind tell me what you know?"

The first jockey reached up a dirty-nailed hand to rub at the back of his neck. "Gibson was down in the tavern last night," he said as though each word were costing him a great deal. "He can get a bit mouthy after he's got a couple of drinks in him."

"That so?" asked Carson lightly, although his stomach had just plummeted into his toes. "He rub someone the wrong way?"

"I reckon he rubbed everyone a bit sideways last night," said the second man. His horse scraped at the dirt with its front hoof. "He was going on and on about how each and every one of us was going to be beaten by a woman in the championships next weekend."

"That's an odd thought," said Carson, frowning. "A woman riding in a race?"

"Well, see, that's what we was all telling him. But Gibson, you know, he could get real worked up about the races. He can get worked up about anything when he's drinking."

"Somebody take a swipe at him? Maybe two?" challenged Carson, looking between the two men.

"Naw," said the first. "He left pretty early."

"Did you see anyone leave after him?" The two men looked at one another again and Carson grimaced. "This'd go a lot quicker if the two of you would be straight with me," he said.

The one on the right grimaced. "Bart Finley can have a bit of a temper on him, even without a drink in him," said one of the men. "You'd find him in the track stables about now, he usually heads in here around the time we finish up."

Carson nodded to them both. "Much obliged," he said.

"I wouldn't...er... I wouldn't be wanted to make him angry!" called the first man to Carson's retreating back. "He's got friends in high places. All over the place, actually."

"I'm sure he and I will have a nice, pleasant chat!" Carson yelled back.

There was a tavern in London that Carson had been talked into entering with a friend once upon a time. It had been a rough and tumble sort of place, lacking every form of class or sophistication that other such establishments had already obtained. Within it he had encountered a group of very unfriendly men. From this group, he'd immediately been able to spot the leader. He was the tallest, the broadest and obviously the strongest of the lot.

With jockeys however, the whole idea seemed to be quite different. Bart Finley was as short a man as they came. Carson would have went so far as to call him the shortest jockey he had ever seen, and that was saying something. He had a squat, unshaven face and two rather large front teeth, which made him look something like an angry beaver. His arms were long and gangly, and there was a stringy quality about him that immediately made Carson's skin crawl. He imagined that this particular individual wasn't incredibly popular with the ladies in New York. Perhaps that was the reason that he looked so very unhappy.

Carson noticed the man as soon as he entered the stables, feeling just as wrong-footed as he had done on that other occasion.

"You would be Bart Finley?"

"Depends on who's asking," said Bart, and he grinned. It was an unfortunate thing to see. On a normal human, any normal human, a smile generally had the effect of making a person look cheerful, or at least more agreeable. That was not the case with Mr. Finley. His grin widened his mouth and displayed two rows of crooked teeth that looked as though they had been knocked out and then glued back in. "What can I do for you, sir? Looking for a rider? A bet? Either way, I'm your guy."

"I have a feeling that you are, Mr. Finley." Carson was staring at the man and thinking idly that he could probably take him on with both hands tied behind his back. "You know a man by the name of Gibson?"

Bart Finley's blotchy face grew even blotchier. "Say, what's this all about?" he said aggressively. "I'm trying to work her, Mister. What's Gibson got to do with any of it?"

"You know him?"

Finley spat on the stable floor between them. "Yeah, I know him. He was in the tavern last night, drunk as a skunk, shouting nonsense at the top of his lungs."

"Really?" asked Carson. "Something that he said offend you a little bit?"

"Pssh, I don't got time to listen to Gibson's sodding mouth. He always talks too much."

"So I've heard," grumbled Carson. He watched Finley pulling on his gloves for a minute. "Gibson's in the hospital right now," he said.

Finley let out a high chuckle. "Serves him right," he said sourly. "Somebody probably got sick of his mouth."

"But if that somebody were... say... another jockey, don't you think there would be an issue there? Perhaps with the benefactor?"

"Get out of it, you!" snarled Finley. "Who asked you to come nosing around?!"

"I have a feeling…" Carson hesitated. "Maybe you had an issue with Gibson? I mean, he's still unconscious. It doesn't look like he'll be fit for next weekend at all."

Bart Finley stepped forward, putting his round beaver-face offensively close to Carson's. "Yeah?" he spat. "You think so, do ya? You think I had something to do with it? Why don't you prove it?!"

Carson took a step back from Finley, and nonchalantly dusted down the front of his jacket. "I do believe," he said, smiling grimly. "That you have just issued me a challenge, sir."

CHAPTER TWELVE

SARAH

"This is all my fault," she whispered. She was sitting beside Gibson's hospital bed, her head hanging low. "I never should have asked him to train me."

"Knowing Gibson, I doubt he gave you much of a choice on the matter," said Carson consolingly.

Sarah's responding laugh was flat and miserable. "I never should have let him do it. What are we going to do? Father is going to have to find a new jockey right before the race. He won't have any time to train on Averleigh."

"What are you talking about, Sarah?" whispered Carson. They were alone in the hospital room. Thomas Brittler was standing out in the hall, conversing in harsh whispers with the doctor. "You were planning on riding in the race," he said.

Sarah turned her eyes onto his handsome face. "Oh, I can't, Carson. Not now. I never should have tried to in the first place."

"But you have to," hissed Carson. "Gibson told me, with you on Averleigh's back, she could win."

"She could just as easily win with someone else riding her," she muttered back.

"But it *should* be you," said Carson. "She's your horse."

Sarah turned away from him and brushed a strand of Gibson's hair away from his bruised and battered face.

"He'd want it to be you," Carson breathed. "Look at him. He risked it all for you to have the chance to ride Averleigh in the championship race. He told me himself, he thought you had a pretty good chance of winning."

"He said that?" Sarah asked. Her heart swelled in her chest and her eyes grew rather misty. "Look at him, Carson. Who would do something like this?"

"His name was Bart Finley," growled Carson.

"You found out? How?" Sarah stammered. She reached across the space between them and grasped Carson's large hand. It was rough and warm, and it encompassed her small hand entirely.

"I went poking around," said Carson with a small shrug. "It was just about as plain as anything. The man had a grudge."

"We have to tell Father," said Sarah, and she made to stand up right then, pushing her chair away from Gibson's bed.

Carson's hand tightened on her own, making her freeze. "We can't," he sighed, and he ran his fingers through his hair in frustration.

"Why on Earth not?" demanded Sarah, her temperature heating.

"Because we don't have any proof," said Carson. "It could have just as easily been a drunken disagreement. He was deep in his cups, according to the other riders. There's no way to prove that it was Finley."

Sarah sank back down into her seat, feeling as though all the air had gone out of her. "We've got to do something," she said. She looked back at Gibson and sighed. Her eyes filled with tears. "This is just so horrible."

"Yes, it is." Sarah jumped. Her father had just rejoined them.

"Poor chap," he said despondently, looking down at Gibson. "Well, I suppose we'll come back and see how he's doing tomorrow. Come on Sarah-Jane, you've been here most of the day. It's time we all had a bite to eat."

Sarah didn't want to leave Gibson all alone. "Hasn't he got a family? Someone we can contact?"

"I'm afraid I don't know, sweetheart," said her father. He gave her shoulder a squeeze. "Come, we'll check on him in the morning."

Sarah cast a miserable glance at Carson, who nodded, and they both got to their feet.

"Miss Sarah?" Gibson's voice was low and weak.

"Gibson," sighed Sarah in relief. She reached for his hand. "What are you doing here?" he asked. "Where are we?"

"You're at the hospital," she told him quietly. "You've had a bit of an accident."

Gibson's eyes were bloodshot and swollen. He looked wretched. "Did I fall off?" he asked slowly. "Was I trampled on the track?"

"Not quite," said Carson.

Her father was waving frantically for a nurse. "He's awake."

"Thank heavens for that," said the nurse, bustling over, wiping her hands on her pinafore as she came. She was a short, plump, kind-faced woman, but she frowned down at her patient with the utmost ferocity. "If you hadn't had your friends here, Mr. Gibson, I don't know that you would have made it back to us."

"But the race," said Gibson drowsily. He sounded befuddled and lost. Sarah gave his calloused hand a squeeze.

"The race hasn't happened yet," she told him kindly.

"Oh good," muttered Gibson, as the nurse brought him a glass of water. "I so wanted to watch."

"Watch?" chuckled Thomas Brittler. "Goodness, but that must have been a hard knock on the head," he said.

Sarah flushed.

They had been intending to make a discreet switch. Gibson was going to ride Averleigh out of the stables towards the track, and on the way, Sarah and he would switch places. But now... she didn't see how that would be possible.

She simply couldn't ride in the race, not without Gibson. If they won, there would be no one to take the award for them. It was too much to hope that her father or anyone else that stood close to her would not recognize her.

"You need to eat," said the nurse, not unkindly, "do you feel like you could have something?"

Gibson nodded painfully, his bloodshot eyes wincing. "'M starving," he said. His voice was hoarse, and Sarah noticed again that imprint on the side of Gibson's face. It was swollen and the skin there was mottled with bruises, but there was no mistaking it. The image was a crest of some sort.

"I'm so very sorry that this happened to you, Gibson," said Sarah.

"Not your fault, Miss," he muttered, leaning up at the nurse began spoon feeding him porridge. He made a face. "That's awful," he said to the nurse.

She smiled. "It could be much worse, Mr. Gibson, now open up."

Gibson's lopsided mouth pulled up in disgust, but he opened he mouth obediently and allowed the nurse to negotiate another bite past his swollen lips.

"I think we'll leave you in peace, Gibson," said her father, and Sarah looked up at him with a frown. "We'll come check on you tomorrow," he added, sternly, catching sight of Sarah's face. "I'm so thankful you've woken up at last. You had us all terrified."

"'M sorry to have caused you all so much trouble," said Gibson.

"No," said Sarah firmly. "No, we're so very sorry Gibson. I'll bring you some pies in the morning, shall I?"

"That would be lovely, Miss," he said, and the callouses on his hand contracted around her small fingers as he gave them a feeble squeeze. "Anything would be better than this mush," he gestured vague fingers at the porridge bowl in the nurse's hand and the woman rolled her eyes to the ceiling. Sarah chuckled and Gibson's bleary gaze focused on her. "You do remind me so very much of my Felicity," he said.

"Who?" asked Carson, bemused.

"My daughter," coughed Gibson. "Felicity, the Miss has a lot of fire in her, just like my little girl did."

Sarah smiled. "Thank you, Gibson," she said, and quietly, she stood to follow her father out of the room, leaving Gibson to grumble good-naturedly over his porridge.

"There's not a way to do it, Mr. Williamson, it simply isn't possible."

It was daybreak, Sarah had led Averleigh out of the livery bright and early, dressed in her riding habit. Carson, for show, had accompanied her. She was now yelling at him through the closed and locked door of the tack room at the racetrack as she struggled out of her dress and into the clothes Gibson had leant her. This time, she had pinned her hair securely in place, and wrapped a bandage so tightly around her bosom that it felt like an unfortunate modification of her stays.

"Then what on Earth are we bothering with all this for?" came Carson's voice. His voice was annoyed.

"Because when father does find someone to replace Gibson, which he will have to do before this next weekend, I won't ever have another chance. Now... I'm coming out, and don't you dare laugh." She opened the door and stepped out into a ray of sunshine that streamed through the high windows.

Carson was leaning casually against the opposite wall, one leg bent back as he chewed nervously on his nails. "If we get caught this time..." he stopped, having just caught sight of Sarah. "Well," he said, looking her up and down. "That's at least better than last time. Where have you put everything?" his eyes were raking her form curiously, as though trying to detect a bulge or a curve.

"Never you mind," said Sarah heatedly. "Can I pass as a man?"

"Maybe a very young boy," said Carson with a shrug. He looked very uncomfortable. "Hold on." He strolled outside and came back with a handful of damp dirt.

"What are you...?"

"Come here," said Carson, and he took her arm and sat her down on a bale of hay. A moment later and he was smearing dirt across Sarah's cheeks. She yelped and leapt back from him.

"That's disgusting," she said, scrubbing at the dirt with the back of her hand. "What did you do that for?"

"You want to be recognizable?" grumbled Carson. "Get back over here and let me finish."

With a sigh, Sarah approached him and stood still with her eyes closed tight.

"There," said Carson after a moment. "That's better. No one will be able to tell that it's you."

"Good," said Sarah. She strolled across the vacant stable and gathered Averleigh's reins into her hands. "Let's go."

Averleigh was on fire. Sarah whooped as her horse went careening past the finish line once again.

"How was that? That had to be her best time, she was flying!"

"Twenty-one seconds," said Carson, clicking the stop watch to reset it. "Not bad. Not bad at all."

"It's fantastic! The horse who won the last race, Nelson? He only averages twenty-five on the quarter." Sarah's head felt light. She slid off her horses back and led Averleigh to the trough. "She could win this thing, you know," said Sarah, seriously. "She could do it."

"You could do it together," said Carson.

"It simply can't happen, Carson. It can't. Not without Gibson." Sarah felt cheated. This had been her only chance. Why did Carson insist on reminding her that it was lost?

"You know," said Carson thoughtfully. "There's every chance we could give everyone a good show. Perhaps Gibson will feel up to it by Saturday."

"What sort of show?" asked Sarah, unable to prevent a small trickle of hope from weaving its way into her heart.

"We would just have to make it look as though Gibson really is capable of riding on Saturday. We could still do the switch. It would be alright." Carson was nodding from the bench beside the commentator's stadium, and Sarah-Jane, looking up at him from the track, was struck anew by how very handsome he was.

"So long as Gibson didn't tumble off Averleigh before we could change places," Sarah said. She scuffed the toe of Gibson's boot in the dirt as Carson trotted down the stairs.

"I could help," he offered hopefully, bending low to peer beneath the brim of Sarah's cap. "I could stay with him all the while."

Sarah sighed. "I suppose we'll just have to wait and see," she said. "But Father's not the type to wait things out, he hates to leave anything to chance. If we don't get to him soon, he'll have another jockey hired before the day is out."

"Well," said Carson, running one hand along his jaw. "We better go and visit Gibson and see what he thinks."

"I'm not going to push him," said Sarah. "I won't do that to him. If he can't do it, that's the end of this, understood?"

Carson frowned at her, and Sarah found herself admiring the wrinkle that formed between his brows as he did so. "Fine," he said at last. "If Gibson can't do it, I'll never mention the idea again, but only on one condition."

It was Sarah's turn to frown at him. "What condition?"

"I would like a kiss," whispered Carson. He grinned in the morning light and held out his arms to her.

Sarah's right eyebrow flew up as she squinted at him. "I don't think so," she said, shaking her head.

"What?" asked Carson suggestively, sauntering over to her and seizing her around the waist. "Don't you want to kiss me Miss Sarah-Jane?"

Sarah squirmed laughing. "Let go of me at once, Mr. Williamson," she cried. "Don't you care what this looks like?"

"What are you talking about?" chuckled Carson, reeling her into his chest.

"I look like a man!" she laughed. "Now release me, you cad, before we're spotted. Otherwise there will soon be some very funny rumors flying around about you, some very funny rumors indeed."

Carson's brow furrowed once more, and then he promptly stepped away from her. "Right then," he said, apparently disturbed. "Let's get you out of those clothes and into something that won't cause New York's society to brand me as a raging lunatic."

Gibson was in far brighter spirits than Sarah had expected him to be. Although his face was still black and blue, he smiled when he saw them approaching.

"Here's my saviors!" he boomed, so loudly that Sarah winced. "You two. I can't thank you enough," Gibson said, wringing each of their fingers in turn. "I would have been in the dead in the gutter without your help."

"It was just lucky we happened to be outside, Gibson," muttered Carson under his breath. "What happened?"

Gibson sobered up at once. "To tell you the truth," he said a little sheepishly. "I'd had quite a bit to drink that night…"

"So we've heard," said Carson. "You made a few enemies in the tavern the other night. Bart Finley being one of them."

"Bart Finley," growled Gibson, and a very ugly look slid over his face. "I should have known it'd have something to do with him. Whoever nabbed me snuck right up on my tail. I never saw them coming at all. Cowards. I could have taken Finley and his ilk on anytime."

"Was there more than one man involved then?" asked Sarah. She sat down in one of the two chairs beside Gibson's bed, laying the tray that she had brought in with her across the end.

Gibson looked affronted. "Of course there was more than one of them," he snapped irritably. "Would take more than Bart Finley to toss me up like this," he gestured to his face with his good arm, the other was wrapped up in a sling. "Well, is the sorry son of a gun sitting in the jailhouse?" he asked, looking between Carson and Sarah.

Sarah glanced up at Carson, who frowned. "We can't prove it was him," he said. "No one saw him attack you, and you didn't see it yourself."

Gibson sighed and slumped back against his pillows. "Figures," he muttered, glaring at a spot on the opposite wall. "Shame, I really fancied heading over to have a peek at old Finley sitting behind bars. Wellpp... Can't be crying over spilled milk," he said matter-of-factly, and he flung his blankets to the side. "You see that nurse around anywhere?" he asked, glancing toward the doorway.

"No," responded Sarah starting to get to her feet. "Should I call her?"

"No, you should not," grumbled Gibson and he swung his legs out of the bed. "Blasted woman won't even let me get up to move around a bit."

"But should you be—?" Carson and Sarah were both watching Gibson with some concern.

"My legs ain't broken, are they? Nothing keeping me from walking around. And..." he added, lowering his voice as he climbed slowly to his feet. "Ain't nothing keeping me from riding on Saturday."

"You see!" cried Carson, beaming down at Sarah. "I knew you'd say that," he said to Gibson. "Miss Sarah is convinced you won't even be able to stay in the saddle long enough to make the switch."

Gibson was tottering shakily toward the far end of the room. Sarah was watching him nervously, ready to leap to her feet if he looked as though he might fall. "Hogwash," said Gibson, turning around to face them both, but ruining the effect by wincing slightly. "I'm fit as a fiddle."

Sarah gazed at him. Her face must have been easy to read because Gibson said, quietly, "There's nothing and no one that could keep me from the track on Saturday. I want to see you win this thing."

Sarah shook her head slowly. "I'll speak to Father," she said, "but unless you put on a better show for him than you just did for us, I can't imagine him allowing you to ride."

Gibson sat down on the edge of his bed, looking sideways at Sarah and Carson. His eyes were narrowed in thought. Then a grin spread slowly over his swollen lips. "Bring him by tomorrow," he said, "I have a plan."

CHAPTER THIRTEEN

CARSON

The next few days sped by. Carson never did discover how Gibson had managed to convince Thomas Brittler that he was well enough to ride in the race. Sarah's father had visited Gibson alone on Tuesday, after which, he raised no objections.

Gibson improved a little as the week wore on, but by Friday afternoon, the day before the race, Sarah was still fussing over him.

"Are you sure you should be doing this?" she asked, as Carson helped Gibson maneuver his stiff shoulder into a fresh shirt behind a changing curtain.

"I'm cleared to leave, aren't I?" came Gibson'a voice, heavily muffled by the collar of his shirt. Carson could hear Sarah pacing up and down the room.

"Yes," she mumbled from the other side of the curtain. "But that doesn't mean cleared to ride. I don't know how we're going to pull this off."

"What'd she say?" asked Gibson as his round, balding head popped out from the depths of cotton.

Carson chuckled. "She's worrying again," he said in an undertone, pulling the shirt to the side so that Gibson could slide his arm into the sleeve.

Gibson winced as he slowly straightened his elbow. "Again?" he said. "When did she stop worrying?"

"You realize that I can hear you, don't you?" came irritated Sarah's voice, and both men laughed. Carson pushed aside the changing curtain and gazed across the cramped room to the place we're Sarah-Jane still paced, wringing her hands.

"It's going to be fine," he said soothingly. "What is there to worry about?"

Sarah glared at him. "Would you like me to order the possibilities from least likely to most likely? Where should I start?"

"How about don't start," said Gibson, coming around the curtain and facing Sarah with a scowl. His bruises were tinged a nasty green now, and his face still looked swollen in places. "We've got it all worked out."

"What if we can't make the switch back?" asked Sarah, sounding terrified. "What if there is too much chaos and you can't get to me?"

Gibson sat down on the edge of his bed facing Sarah and the doorway. "Everything will be fine, Miss. Settle yourself down. Remember why you wanted to do this in the first place?"

Carson watched Sarah's shoulders relax. "I know," she whispered. "There's just so much that could go wrong."

Carson rolled up Gibson's clothes and stuffed them into a burlap sack. "Nothing will go wrong if we stick to the plan," he said, and he came right up to Sarah and took hold of her hand, ignoring the fact that Gibson was watching. "We can do this," he whispered to her. "If this is what you want, we'll make this happen."

Sarah looked at him, long and hard, as though she was deciding whether or not to trust him. At last, she smiled, and her entire face seemed to light up from within. She was so beautiful. "Yes," she whispered, "yes, I want this."

"Good," growled Gibson, "so there'll be no more fuss about it. Remember the plan, and I'll see you both to-morrow."

Life in the Brittler house was more or less the same as life in his own house, with a few significant changes. First,

Sarah-Jane was a glowing, incandescent beam of light that made the rooms sparkle when she entered them. If she took him unawares, as she had multiple times, it took Carson's eyes a little while adjust.

Secondly, laughter often rang out from any room where the Brittler sisters were congregated, and their laughter always had a way of making him suspect that he was the subject of their amusement.

The Brittler's summer estate was bright and airy, with a warmth that bordered on suffocating, or perhaps that was simply the amount of people that resided within it. Carson had always been used to a large house, but he had never lived in one that was full of people. It had always been him and his father, just the two of them, and a handful of servants. Here, anywhere that he went, apart from his bedroom, was already occupied. Thomas Brittler frequented the study. Mrs. Brittler enjoyed the parlor room, while the girls seemed to enjoy floating around the small kitchen and teasing their cook, Marcia.

It took very few days for Carson to feel perfectly at home. The house was busier than his own, but at least he wasn't suffering from constant headaches caused by dust and hammering. Then of course, the best part was Sarah-Jane. The more time he spent in her company, the deeper he fell under her spell. He wondered if she could see how she effected him.

When she walked into a room, he sat up straight. When she spoke, his ears pricked at the sound of her voice. He was rapidly becoming obsessed with her, but she didn't seem to mind one bit.

The Friday night before the big race, a strange calm seem to come over Sarah. It was as though she had solidified somehow. Carson kept stealing glances to the place where she sat next to him at the dinner table, waiting for a sign or a signal that would tell him it was time to act.

It was always here that he had trouble keeping his hands to himself. She was so close to him that he could smell her. She smelled of chardonnay. Exquisite and rich and delightful, each time that he inhaled Carson found his fingers aching to stroke her skin.

"You'll be joining us for the race tomorrow, won't you, Mr. Williamson?"

"What?" Carson looked around. Mrs. Brittler was speaking to him. "Oh, yes, of course I will," he said with a smile. "Should be quite enjoyable," Sarah flashed him a wicked grin. He couldn't help himself. He slid his hand beneath the table cloth and reached for her as he casually took a drink from his glass. Her slight intake of breath made him shiver the tiniest bit. He hoped that no one had noticed.

"I say, my dear," said Thomas from the head of the table, fixing his eyes on Sarah. "You're looking rather flushed. Are you quite well?"

Sarah patted her cheeks. "Actually," she said quietly, "I'm feeling a bit dizzy. I think I might have to call it a night."

Carson withdrew his hand reluctantly as Sarah made to stand up. When she stumbled, he flew out of his seat.

"Miss Sarah? Are you alright?"

"I'm fine. I'm sure I'm just overtired," she said, smiling up at him. She looked it. In fact, Carson wasn't quite convinced that all of this was an act. A little extra sleep before the strain of tomorrow would doubtless do her some good. Carson glanced at Sarah's plate as she exited the room and made a mental note to smuggle her a bit of extra food. She would need her strength for the race.

He might have been imagining it, but he thought Thomas Brittler looked a little smug as he said: "sleep well, my dear. I'm sure you'll feeling better in the morning."

"Goodnight," Sarah called weakly to her family, and the dining room door closed softly behind her.

"Sarah?" Carson knocked softly on her bedroom door an hour later. He could still hear the sound of laughter and voices echoing from down the hall, so he knew the rest of the family was safely ensconced in the drawing room.

"Carson?" her voice was sleepy, as though she had indeed crawled into bed although it was only six-thirty. He hoped he hadn't woken her.

"I brought you something to eat," he whispered to the doorframe. "Open up."

There was the sound of soft footsteps, a rustle, and then the doorknob turned. "Thank heavens," she said under her breath, "I'm absolutely starving, I was so nervous I forgot to eat at dinner."

"I noticed," said Carson. He was averting his eyes. Sarah was wearing a robe over a lacy nightdress. He could just see the side of her pretty face through the crack in the door, and it was all he could do to keep himself from shoving the door open and flinging himself on her.

He glanced up as she opened the door a bit wider to reach for the plate he held in his hands, and then he looked quickly down again.

Sarah laughed. "Mr. Williamson, you've seen me in trousers a handful of times, but never before have I seen you this color of scarlet."

Carson cleared his throat uncomfortably. "Perhaps you should close the door," he said hoarsely.

She did, but the closed door did not disguise her giggles. "Oh, Mr. Williamson," she called as he turned away.

"Yes?"

"Thank you," she breathed.

Carson's heart was throbbing painfully in his chest when he laid down to sleep that night. He lay awake for hours, staring at the ceiling and imagining Sarah-Jane curled up next to him in the dark.

Sarah

"Darling, you look positively dreadful," said her mother. Sarah shrugged as she tugged on the strings of her stays, pulling them snug and tying them in a neat bow at her navel. "Are you sure you should be out of bed? You're still very flushed."

"I'm fine, Mother," she snapped. "Would you mind helping me into my dress?"

Samantha approached her, looking wary. "Your father isn't going to like this," she said, doing up the buttons of

Sarah's blue gown with practiced ease. "Look at you, your clammy all over."

This was quite true. Sarah had purposely stood beside her window for several minutes before the rest of the family had awoken, letting the cold morning air dampen her skin, then she'd pinched her cheeks into a fine rose red.

"I'm not missing this race," she said defiantly, and she strolled to her dressing table and began running a brush gingerly through her hair.

Her mother sighed. "Let me do that, dear," she said. Sarah felt her mother's warm fingers her own as she pulled the brush from them, and she looked up at her, feeling unaccountably tender.

"Thank you," she whispered. Guilt writhed in her gut like a pit of angry snakes. If she were caught... but the game was in motion. She had already made her choice. There was no going back now.

"I know how much it means to you to be there today," said Samantha as she smoothed the coarse bristles through Sarah's hair. "But it's not really worth you risking your health, is it?"

Sarah smiled. "I'll be alright, Mother, truly I will be."

"Alright," said Samantha. She began pinning Sarah's hair into an elegant knot on the top of her head, "just don't be surprised if your father puts his foot down."

Sarah sighed. If her father didn't try to stop her from going, she would have to think of some other means of excusing herself. But she needn't have worried.

"Absolutely not!" her Father's voice was so loud that Sarah's heart skipped a beat. "No, no. I'm sorry, but you'll just have to sit this one out, dear. Look at you. You can hardly stand. You're not going."

Sarah glared at her father. "Father, please, I just need to—."

"No!" growled Thomas. "And that's my final word."

Sarah tried not to look victorious as each member of her family passed her on the way out of the front door.

"I'll stay back with her," said Dianna. She looked particularly distressed.

"No, no," said Sarah, waving her hand irritably. "You go on. I'll want a blow by blow account of the race when you return, so you better take notes."

Dianna frowned. "Charlotte could do it..."

"No," said Sarah. "Look, it's a brilliantly sunny day. I'm not going allow it to be spoiled for everyone. You all go and have fun. That includes you Mr. Williamson," she said, wagging a finger at him as he opened his mouth to speak. "I'll see you all later."

Sarah cast Carson a small wink as he made to follow after her sisters. He smiled and mouthed: "Good luck."

All of them glanced back at her before they climbed into the carriage. Sarah waved, doing her best to look downright miserable while her excitement was building up in her chest like a tidal wave.

She closed the door as the carriage set off, her heart about to leap out of her throat. It was time.

After telling Marcia—who she knew would relay the information to the rest of the household—that she was going back to bed, Sarah shut herself in her room and locked the door behind her.

She had stashed an exact replica of Gibson's racing uniform in her carpet bag the night before, and now, with trembling fingers, Sarah tugged it free. Today, it was more important than ever that she was not recognized. She had to hide everything. Her hair would be the most difficult part, Gibson wore his trimmed short, and his hair was dark. Sarah, with her normally dark hair lightened by the sun, would be instantly recognizable if her cap were to fly off.

Sarah glared at her reflection in the mirror for a few moments, and then she started to undress. She was pressed for time, and that made her clumsy. As she yanked on her riding boot, she stumbled backward and landed with a thud inside her open wardrobe. Gowns cascaded down on her head, engulfing her in lace and frills.

It took Sarah much longer than she had hoped it would. By the time she had shoved everything back in her wardrobe, she was running very late.

She glanced at the clock on her bedside table. It was a quarter past noon. The race would start at one. She needed to get there. Sarah turned to face her mirror again. Her eyes were wide and she could see her pulse pounding against the thin skin of her throat.

She unwrapped the blue kerchief that Gibson had given her and tied it fast around her face. Then with her mouth scrunched, she reached into her bag and withdrew the small tin of powdered charcoal that Carson had given her.

Gibson's face was covered in bruises, so hers had to look as though it was too. She dabbed the charcoal on, holding her breath. She hoped it didn't stain, but there was no way to get around the fact.

She tucked the tin back into her bag and stood up. That'd have to do. She doubted anyone would be paying enough attention to her to notice more than the speed of the horse she rode. Smiling, her heart still thrumming, Sarah threw open her window and slid out of it into the hedgerow.

Chapter Fourteen

THE CROWDS THRONGING THE race track were so thick that Sarah was able to slide through them without being noticed. Her breathe was sharp in her throat, and her pulse was pounding in her ears.

The path leading from the stables to the starting line had been mercifully cordoned off, but she hadn't banked on the two men striding up and down it. Security of some sort. Terrified, her face hot from the sun, Sarah dithered on the spot wondering what to do.

Then miraculously, Carson was there. "Wait," he whispered in her ear, and then he slid past her, his fingers brushing over her waist.

Sarah watched Carson's immaculate body part the crowd with ease. He approached one of the men, gesturing wildly at the far side of the stands. The second patroller joined the first, and they both set off at a run. Carson glanced up to the place where Sarah stood and gave her a nod and the shadow of a wink.

Sarah peered around and then strolled casually up the path. Once she was around the corner and out of sight, she darted beneath the stands and waited, her breathing ragged and her chest tight with anxiety. She watched, carefully keeping out of sight, as the crowd thinned. People were filing into the stands over her head. She could hear laughter and snatches of what sounded like singing.

A few moments later, she heard the sound of the gong. Betting was closed, it was time for the audience to take their seats. Sarah turned her attention to the path just beside her. The gloves she wore were making her palms moist. Her hands were balled into fists. The first jockey appeared on the back of Nelson, the winner of the last race. Then came the second, and the third, trotting past the place where Sarah crouched, ready, waiting. Averleigh trotted around the corner last, Gibson clinging to her back and wincing as he did so. Sarah slid quietly out of the stands and helped Gibson to the ground. "Thank you," she whispered to him, hoping her voice wasn't trembling as bad as her hands.

"Good luck, Miss," he said. "I'll be watch through the gaps and I'll be waiting right here as soon as the race is over."

Sarah nodded and scrambled into the saddle as Gibson slid beneath the stands, then, her hands shaking, she trotted Averleigh onto the track.

The crowd screamed as they took their place beside the other riders, none of whom looked at her. They were all engrossed in their own mounts. Sarah ran her hands nervously over the pins holding her cap in place and bent low, feeling Averleigh's reassuring heat beneath her. "Are you ready?" she whispered in her ear. "We can do this."

Sarah ran over the things that Gibson had told her over the last few weeks, and the knowledge that she could remember every single one of his riding tips was a strange source of comfort. Her hands tightened on the reins as the second gong rang out. She could just hear the commentator shouting to be heard over all the noise.

The crowd grew quiet and Sarah grew still. She felt Averleigh's muscles tense beneath her. She was trying not to hold her breath.

The gun shot sounded. Sarah kicked Averleigh forward. Jockeys were yelling, the spectators were screaming, but it was all meaningless noise to Sarah. Averleigh's hooves were pounding into the track, and her heart had begun to sing.

Averleigh loved to *run.* Her horse pulled on the reins as Sarah held her in check. *Not too soon, not too soon.* They rounded the first bend on the outside just behind Nelson and Liberty Bell, whose black pelt was shining in the sun. Sarah loosened the reins a bit. Averleigh picked up speed. She urged her horse into the midst of the other horses, riding alongside Dagger's Point, and then she was passing him.

Clouds of dirt were smothering her vision. Sarah squinted as they sailed past the starting point. The crowd a brief roar in her ears. Three more laps. Averleigh was holding steady, they were right in the middle. It was time to pull forward.

"Yah!" Sarah shouted, digging in her heels, and Averleigh began climbing. As they rounded the final bend, she swiped at her eyes. Sweat was beading on her forehead. Averleigh had scooted past Gambit on the inside and she was hot on Bell's tail. They were on the third lap, holding place, and Liberty Bell began falling behind.

As they shot past the start line for the third time, Sarah gave a whoop and Averleigh sped up again. But her horse was tiring. She and Nelson were neck and neck. Sarah saw Nelson's jockey glance at her, saw his eyes go wide. "Come on. Come on!" Sarah was chanting. And they were rounding the final turn. Averleigh was snorting and huffing, her hooves scraping at the track. Sarah kept her head down as they flew past the finish line, unable to tell who was in the lead. Had they done it?

Nelson's jockey was cursing fluently beside her as their horses slowed. Sarah kept her eyes averted. The crowd was screeching from the stands, half of them were on their feet, and Sarah felt a sudden leap of terror. She trotted Averleigh in a circle, her eyes scanning the space beneath the stands for Gibson as the other riders slowed beside them.

"What are you playing at?!" shouted the jockey from her left. Sarah turned to look at him. He was a tiny man with crooked teeth and the face of a beaver. His squinting eyes were scanning her face in fury as he slid from Nelson's back. The man tossed his cap onto the ground, staring up into her face.

Sarah remembered the way his eyes had widened as he gazed at her on the track. Had he realized that she wasn't Gibson?!

Sarah clambered from Averleigh's back, her eyes darting around for an escape. She took hold of Averleigh's reins as the furious little man made to stride around her and negotiated her horse out of the bedlam surrounding them, towards the path that led to the stables.

There he was. Gibson was waving at her frantically. Sarah's breathing uneven. She glanced around, made sure that they were carefully hidden from sight by Averleigh's massive bulk, and then skittered into the space beneath the stands. Gibson said nothing to her as he took her place. He strolled alongside Averleigh confidently, looking as cool as you please, bringing her about so that he could face the chaos that was the racehorses and their riders.

Sarah could just hear the commentator shouting into his speaking trumpet. "Quiet, please! Ladies and gentleman, the standings are clear!" The man sounded jovial.

The squat man who looked like a beaver had located Gibson at last. Gibson was looking heartily amused as the tiny jockey sputtered at him. He was staring at Gibson, obviously flummoxed.

"Riders?! Please line your mounts along the start line."

Sarah scrambled around so that she could get a good view through a crack in the boards. Gibson strolled beside Averleigh, pulling down the blue handkerchief he had tied around his face. Sarah saw that he looked just as disheveled as the rest of them. He'd taken no chances. There were even spots of dirt and grime spattering his bruised cheeks. Sarah wondered whether Carson had tossed dirt at him.

A hand came down across Sarah's mouth and she let out a muffled cry. She spun around, ready to fight off her assailant, but it was only Carson.

"Mr. Williamson," she said, putting a hand to her chest and attempting to catch her breath. "Must you insist on—?"

"You were brilliant!" he hissed. "You were fantastic. Neck and neck there in the end with Finley, but you caught him."

Sarah beamed excitedly. "It wasn't me. It was Averleigh. But who won? I couldn't see...? He was so close to us."

"Shh," whispered Carson, putting a finger to his lips. "They're about to announce the winner. Look."

Sarah tugged the blue handkerchief—the one that was identical to Gibson's—away from her face and began to wipe the charcoal away from her eyes as she spun to face the track. She didn't even protest as Carson's thick arms encircled her waist. Her whole body was vibrating with excitement.

"The winner," said the commentator, who had come down from the stands to stand beside the racers on the track. "By just a head, is clearly our very own Averleigh of Manhattan, who belongs to Sarah-Jane Brittler!"

Sarah shrieked and Carson clapped a hand to her mouth, but it hardly mattered. The stands had exploded with noise. Clapping and cheering and a few boos from those who had bet on Nelson to win. Sarah couldn't contain herself. She began to cry, and as the tears poured down her face she spun around and kissed Carson, who responded with gusto, lifting Sarah a few inches off the ground.

Carson

The noise around them faded as Sarah pressed her mouth to his. She was something of a mess. The upper half of her face was still smudged with charcoal, and tears were streaming down her cheeks. But he reveled in her joy, and in the taste of her lips against his.

There was the sound of shouting from the field. Sarah twisted back around to stare at the scene that was unfolding.

"He's a cheat!" Finley was shouting at the top of his lungs. "A cheat!!"

"Now we don't really like sore losers, do we?" muttered Carson. He'd been watching Finley with intensity before he was so thoroughly distracted by Sarah-Jane. "I'll be right back."

The crowd was all watching Finley, shaking their heads. Finley was pointing a dirty-nailed finger at Gibson, who was smiling.

Carson approached the group quietly. He could feel hundreds of eyes following him from the stands. "Speaking of cheats," he said in Finley's ear and he grabbed the man's arm as he started forward, readying himself to take a swing at Gibson.

"Would you mind if I had a look at that ring you're wearing, Finley?"

"What..?" Finley was too slow to stop Carson as he lifted his right hand and plucked a gold ring from his middle finger.

"Say, what's this all about?" grumbled the commentator, striding forward. "Mr. Finley, calm yourself at once, or I shall have you escorted from the track."

"Sir," said Carson, releasing his hold on Finley. "Our jockey was attacked last week by Mr. Finley, and possibly a few accomplices."

The commentator looked taken aback.

"Until now, we had no way of proving Mr. Finley's involvement, but..." he beckoned Gibson over to them, who came, still grinning. "Mr. Gibson, could you show us the bruising on your left cheek?"

Gibson obliged, turning his face to display the ugly mark that Finley's ring had made in his flesh. Carson held out the ring to the commentator, who took it and held it up to the mark.

"Disqualified!!" he cried vehemently.

"What?!" bawled Finley, staring around. "That's not mine!"

Two men moved forward, and Carson recognized them as the security men he had distracted so that Sarah could slip into her hiding place. Neither of them glanced twice at Carson, however, as they took hold of Mr. Finley's arms and began shunting him off the track.

"No! Cheat! Cheat! He's a cheat!" he cried, digging in his heels. But Finley was so small that the two men holding him merely shrugged and seized his feet at well.

Still shouting at the top of his lungs, Finley was carried bodily from the track."

"Apologies folks!" the Commentator shouted as Carson nodded and stepped to the side. "There has been a little change in the line up. Second place, along with its ribbons and prize money, will fall to Gambit of Broomshaven, owned by Mr. Grimsby! And third place to Liberty Bell..." But Carson had stopped listening.

He had just seen Sarah slinking away in the distance, and he smiled, strolled off the track and ran to rejoin her family. He would see her at home.

CHAPTER FIFTEEN

SARAH

The journey back to her family's summer cottage seemed the easiest thing in the world after that. Sarah kept her head down and meandered through the streets, listening to the cheers of the crowd around the track growing quieter and quieter with the distance.

She had stayed just long enough to watch Averleigh bestowed with a wreath of roses and then she had been forced to leave silently, fighting the urge to jump into the air and whoop. They had done it. Against all odds. Against everything that was thrown their way, they had done it. She and Averleigh and Gibson and even Carson. They had won together, and Finley had been disqualified. That was the cherry on top of the cake if there ever was one.

Sarah slipped back in through her window and looked around at her room. It was as though she had been expecting it to look different somehow, but it didn't. The bed still sat against the far wall, looking warm and inviting. The sheer curtains around the windows waved in lazy acknowledgment as if to say: "Hey, you're back. We forgot you had left."

Yes, things would be very much the same, even after the summer had ended and the Brittler's had returned to Manhattan once more. Nothing would have changed in Sarah's life. She would still be the well-bred daughter of a wealthy steel merchant. She would still have her sisters by her side. Her mother would still be attempting to marry her off to Carson... Sarah paused on that thought, freezing in the act of pulling the window closed.

Carson. She smiled, picturing his handsome face, and the way he liked to hold her in secret. As if he owned her and it was a contract acknowledged only between the two of them. In front of everyone else it was Miss Sarah-Jane this or that, but when they were alone... he liked to call her Sarah.

Sighing and stretching, she started to undress. The stiff bandages around her upper body had left indents around her ribs, and she was eager to wash the black marks from her face. She rang for her housemaid and requested a hot bath through her closed bedroom door and an hour later, she sank to her neck in the hot suds.

If someone had asked her months ago if she would have liked to ride Averleigh to victory this summer, she would have said yes in a heartbeat, knowing that it could never happen. But it had happened. Not only had she been able to ride her horse at the Brighton Beach racecourse, (something that had never once been done before by a woman) she had *won*. At this moment, right now, Sarah was the happiest girl in the world. She had lived a dream that wasn't possible, and now... now she was hungry and in desperate need of a nap.

When her family returned home, Sarah pretended to have enjoyed a refreshing nap and long hot bath. Her eyes were still ringed in tiredness, so it was not very difficult to play the part of an invalid.

Her sisters sat her down in the drawing room with a cup of hot soup, each of them talking a mile a minute.

Noelle had bounded onto the house with the largest trophy Sarah had ever seen, and she'd beamed as Sarah had burst into tears.

"She did it!"

"She was gorgeous, Sarah!"

"I can't believe it! She was amazing!"

"She snapped it up right at the very end," said her mother, smiling fondly at her. "It was really very impressive."

Just then, her father entered the room. Behind him came Carson, and his eyes seemed to light up as they fell on her.

"Averleigh's out in the yard," said Thomas. He was examining Sarah's tear stained face with the utmost pride, "and I've signed for your winnings."

Sarah climbed slowly to her feet. She felt drained. Her body was exhausted from all the tension. "Can I see her?" she asked weakly.

"Of course you can," said Thomas and, still beaming, he placed an arm around her back and escorted her out into the yard.

As Sarah approached her horse, she began to cry all over again. She took Averleigh's young, sweet nose into her hands and kissed it. "You were brilliant," she whispered to her. "Absolutely stunning."

"Her rider was very proficient as well." It was her father's voice. Sarah turned to look at him. He was smiling. His eyes were crinkled in amusement and his great, bushy mustache was bristling. As Sarah watched him, she saw a tear glistening at the corner of his eye as well.

Puzzled, she released Averleigh and turned around to face him fully. As she did, her father took a step forward and raised his fingers to the corner of her nose. He scrubbed his thumb lightly over the skin there, and then grinning he said: "you missed a spot."

EPILOGUE

SARAH-JANE SAT ON THE edge of her bed staring blankly at the far wall. It was early afternoon. All around her, the house was in a flurry of activity. She could hear the house-maids walking from room to room gathering suitcases and whispering about which rooms they would close up first.

The summer was fading, the racing season had ended, it was time to go home. With a melancholy sigh, she stretched her arms over her head and glanced towards her bedroom window. Outside, the Brittler's family carriage beckoned, the harnesses jingling slightly as the horses shifted their feet, and a lone horse stood tied against the fence railings on the other side of the yard.

There came a knock on the door. "Sarah?" It was Dianna.

"Come in," Sarah called. She glanced up as her sister entered the room.

"Are you packed?"

"Yes," sighed Sarah. She climbed to her feet, straightening her skirts and cast a weary eye over her empty wardrobe.

Dianna approached her, smiling sadly. "He's getting ready to leave," she whispered.

"Already?" Sarah gasped, startled.

Dianna held the door open for her as she darted out into the hall.

She found Carson Williamson in the parlor with her father. "You're leaving?" she squeaked on entering.

The two men peered up from something on the writing desk.

"What?" asked Carson, looking around. "Oh, yes, Miss Sarah-Jane. We were just tidying things up."

"Why?" Sarah was making no effort to disguise her disappointment.

Her father cleared his throat uncomfortably and straightened up. "I'm just going to see to the last of my things," he muttered and he strolled out of the open parlor door, determinedly avoiding Sarah's eyes.

Carson moved over to Sarah and took her hands in his. A small jolt went through her at his touch. "Why what?" he asked, smiling down at her.

"Why are you leaving?"

He chuckled. "If I recall it correctly, you didn't want me here in the first place." Sarah glared at him. "Clearly, your opinion of me has changed," he added smugly.

"The rest of us aren't leaving for another couple of hours," she said. "Stay for lunch, won't you?"

"I really should be going," said Carson. He gave her fingers a little squeeze and then released her. Sarah felt bereft without his hands on hers as she watched Carson gathering the papers on the desk. "I've trespassed on your family's hospitality quite enough this summer."

"So, where's the harm in trespassing a bit more?" she pleaded.

Her heart was hammering in her chest. Just a little more time, that was all she needed, and then he could go. She could face him leaving after lunch. She didn't want to have to say goodbye just yet.

Carson was shaking his head, still grinning, so Sarah changed tact at top speed. "You've convinced father to invest then, have you?" she said, looking at the papers in his hands.

Carson smiled. "I must confess, I was surprised," he said. "He rather forced the money on me."

"Yes, he can be quite pushy sometimes," said Sarah fondly.

Carson rolled his eyes to the ceiling. "I don't know anyone like that," he said sarcastically.

Sarah ignored him. "Is that it then? It's time to move forward with the hotel?"

"Almost," said Carson. He slid the stack of papers into a briefcase and snapped it closed.

"What happens next?"

"Next?" Carson paused in the act of pulling on his overcoat and peered at her. "Next, I have to secure the property, inform the investors, and begin the process of acquiring building permits." He paused again. "Why are you so curious?"

Sarah shrugged. Although she was highly interested in Carson's plans for the future, her interest today revolved around the possibility of delaying Carson's departure. She ran her fingers over the writing desk and moved closer to Carson, who was watching her, his eyes alight.

"How is the construction on your house?"

"Nearly finished," he said. He was still watching her. One hand scrubbed through his dark hair as he seemed to wither slightly. "I shall only have to endure another week or so."

"You could come with us," she said suddenly, her eyes lighting up.

"What? To Manhattan?"

"Just for another couple of weeks."

Carson laughed again. Sarah frowned at him.

"I've been in your home for almost a month. No," he gathered his briefcase into his arms. "No, I can't ask your parents to host me another moment. Let alone in Manhattan. I need to be here while I move things forward and monitor my father's dealings on this end."

Sarah tried not to sound petulant as she leaned towards him. "Surely there's no harm in staying with us for another couple weeks?"

Carson seemed to be struggling with himself. He stared at her, his eyes roving over her face and sliding down the front of her dress. Then he blinked. "No," he said firmly, turning resolutely away from her.

Sarah moved closer to him, smiling coyly. "I wonder, Mr. Williamson," she said, toying with the buttons on her bodice, "whether you might at least grant me a favor before you leave."

"A favor?" Carson closed the distance between them and scooped her into his arms. "Just one favor?" He kissed her feverishly. "My darling," he whispered. "I would give you the world."

"Then stay," Sarah breathed, her chest constricting. "Stay with me."

Carson groaned. "I won't be very far away," he said.

"But I very much like having you just down the hall," whined Sarah.

"Perhaps, one day," said Carson, smiling down at her in a self-satisfied way. "You might consider sharing a home with me?"

"Carson Williamson, if that is a proposal, it is positively horrid," laughed Sarah, struggling out of his grip.

"No, you go," she giggled as he reached for her again. "Come back to me when you've learned how to do it properly."

Carson laughed, allowing his hand to fall to his side. "Very well," he said. "But will you grant *me* the favor of your company? Perhaps next week? May I come to call?"

"Of course you may," sighed Sarah, "but only if you stay for lunch this afternoon!"

Carson shook his head as Sarah took his hand and began tugging him out of the room.

"Oh, very well," he groaned.

And Sarah, grinning victoriously, led Carson out of the parlor, down the hall and into the dining room, her heart so full of joy she thought it might burst.

The End

There's more to come! Stay up to date by signing up for Josephine Blake's Newsletter
and recieve a FREE copy of *The Heart of Hope-A Brittler Sisters Prequel.*

ABOUT THE AUTHOR

JOSEPHINE BLAKE IS A *USA Today* Bestselling Author and an Award-Winning Graphic Designer. She enjoys a quiet life on a comfortable piece of property in her very own small-town in the Willamette Valley.

With over 20 published books in the romance genre, Josephine works hard to make sure her stories bring a little more love into this crazy world.

She and her husband spend most days chasing their little one around their farmhouse with thankful hearts.

Notable Works:

Josephine Blake's debut Historical Romance novel, *Dianna*, hit the shelves in August of 2016 and became a bestseller two years later. Her Gothic Historical Romance novel, *A Brush with Death*, followed suit later that year in 2018. Yours at Yuletide became her very first Contemporary Romance release in the winter of 2019.

Sign Up for her newsletter to stay up to date on every new release at www.awordfromjosephineblake.com.

ALSO BY JOSEPHINE BLAKE

The Brittler Sisters Series

Dianna

Little Rose

Charlotte

Sarah-Jane

Noelle

The Heart of Hope

The Brides of Adoration

Maid in the West

Cowboy, Take Me Away

The Arms of a Stranger

Nursing His Heart

JOSEPHINE BLAKE

Sweet Love of Mine
Brenden's Bookish Bride

–◇–

Love in Unity Springs
Yours at Yuletide
Second-Chance Santa
Mistletoe Miracles
Candy-Cane Kisses
Christmas in Unity Springs-Series Collection

–◇–

Standalones
Two Hearts, One Stone

–◇–

Multi-Author Projects
The ABC Mail Order Brides-Emeline's Exile